I0828617

Book Cover by Yoko Molotov

Proofread by Camilla Harlowe at www.camillaharlowe.com

Contents

Glossary

Dhugaren Terms

Furkurra- a layered casserole

Fortswap- street food similar to pita chips

Urgruffuh- Guardian warriors; often someone who has passed on, like a guardian angel.

Purkull- nocturnal cougar-like carnivorous species on Dhugar

Wursplat- round, furry animal grown like cattle on Dhugar

Winged-One Terms

Battran- flying creatures from their Bejkarr like flying squirrels

Dopticana- stringed instrument

Pyongo- traditional style of bread

minkla- baby mobiles, carves with crystals

Nifir- glowing crystals

Infinium- courting statues, carved by Winged-One males for their chosen mate.

Silfan Terms

Dersials- large insects that are a popular snack on Sanctuary Station

Sprimin- Silfan's version of guardian angels

Falofon- instrument like a guiro, used to lull dersials

Ferziti Terms

Subus- a hot, caffeinated drink, similar to coffee

Prologue

Congratulations! You have been selected to become a citizen of Sanctuary Station. Sanctuary Station is an initiative created by the Originem to foster community, sustainability, and innovation. Integrating over a dozen species from across the galaxy, all descended from ancestral Originem colonies founded over a million years ago, our space station is the safest, most diverse, and most prosperous place to live in the galaxy.

As you have learned over the last year on your "jump-start" satellite, humans are one of many races that call the Milky Way galaxy home. In fact, over thirty species have joined the Intergalactic Relations Association, and at least eighty percent of these species have been definitively proven to be descendants of the Originem.

Like many other Sanctuary Station residents, your home planet has been made uninhabitable by mass flooding caused by global warming. Due to the misuse of your home planet and its resources, planet-side privileges for humans have been suspended for five hundred years. We are sorry for your loss.

In this video we'll go over various facets of life on Sanctuary Station. First, let's talk about navigation. Our Station is divided into divisions, and those into subdivisions. You'll find your apartment address listed by three numbers: first your division number, then sub number, then lastly your own apartment number. Elevators are located in the center of each division and have helpful navigational boards in the corridors.

Sanctuary Station is kept on a twenty five hour day schedule. Twenty Five hours is considered the appropriate compromise for all our citizens, whose home planets have rotations from twenty two to thirty hours. You will notice that the lighting in public areas will be dimmed or brightened to signify the time of day. As stated previously, Sanctuary Station is the safest place in the galaxy, so even when lights are low, you can feel secure walking around your new home.

Each apartment is equipped with nutritional printers. These have been programmed with several popular meals from each species represented on our station. We encourage you to experiment with new foods and cultures. All citizens are tested for allergies before arrival and the nutritional printers in their apartments will be programmed with this information. Sequence codes for all pre-programmed human meals and a sampling of meals from other species have been included at the end of this orientation video.

1

Hope

There's something suspicious about the Originem. What kind of people build a whole, planet-sized space station and let refugees live there for free? Not to mention, I think I'm the only person who noticed most of the humans invited to live here are young, single women.

The most suspicious thing I've noticed here on Sanctuary Station, though, is its distinct lack of art. After 3 whole days on this space station, I still have not found one drawing utensil, not one sketchpad or even a pencil. Everyone tells me that's what the datapads are for, but clearly they are not artists. Digital art is simply not the same—especially to someone as tech-inept as I am. I used to think my sister, Prudence, was an artist, but she keeps telling me to chill and calling this place a utopia. So it seems like I might be the only traditional artist left in this screen-obsessed *dys*topia.

I followed Prue here, and I have no regrets. My sister and I have to stick together, after all—but I was never sold on the whole "community-minded" spiel they were selling. I thought it sounded kinda cult-y, honestly. And looky here, it's been only three days and I've already discovered a crack in their perfect community. How can you have a community, anyways, when you don't have art? No murals, no personality. This is simply a fact.

This train of thought is what leads me here, in a darkened corridor, in the middle of "the sleep cycle." Like everyone didn't already have a perfectly good word for "night" in their native tongue. See? Suspicious.

I pull on my makeshift ski mask, a stretched out tube sock with some creative cuts and knots, and peruse my collection of aerosol spray cans and the canvas of blank metal wall in front of me. My plan is risky. Prue might even call it harebrained. She's been scarce since this morning, though, so I haven't had someone to spitball my ideas off of. Or to vent my frustration. Really, she is as responsible for what is about to happen as I am.

With that invigorating thought, I choose my first can, shaking it vigorously and mapping my piece in my mind. Then, with a pressurized hiss, I get to work. I really should be wearing something over my eyes, but this is kind of last minute as far as plans go. At least my mouth and nose are somewhat covered by the sock and the hallways are wide and tall. The dim lights and the quiet hum of mechanical things set a tranquil scene for painting.

As with all new projects, the first few strokes are shaky ones. Painting—art in general—is not like riding a bike for me. Every time I start something new, I have to relearn everything. As always, though, after twenty minutes or so, I find my groove again and then it's like a dance I've forgotten the steps to, but my body remembers.

As I work, I let all the frustration slowly ooze out of me and onto my makeshift metal canvas. The last three days, I've been so lonely and restless. Prue is usually my ride or die. Back in Cincinnati, we did everything together. When we were rescued by the Originem, dying of dehydration while surrounded by dirty, brackish water on the roof of our apartment building, we swore to each other that we'd never let them separate us. It turns out, they never wanted to.

It really does seem too good to be true. Benevolent alien overlords who want to set us up with everything we need and hang out braiding each other's hair? I've read enough science fiction to know that somewhere there's a curtain, and behind it, there's a human meat market or an alien petting zoo, or something else fucky going on. Well, peel it back because they obviously mean to suck the life out of us until we're too dispirited to fight back when they start auctioning us off.

Luckily, I'm here now to bring a little life to this place and save everyone here from a terrible fate. You're welcome, alien neighbors.

In Cincinnati, I had a graffiti phase, so I'm having no problem wielding these aerosol cans with a little bit of skill, once I modified their nozzles. This morning I was bored enough to start cleaning our already spotless apartment with an assortment of cleaners I found in a utility closet on the main corridor. When I saw the chrome countertop in our kitchen develop a green tinge to it reminiscent of the coppery-green color of old pennies, I nearly wept. I'd made a mess of our countertops finding all the reactive chemical cleaners and memorizing their shades, then I hunted down a tube sock, made it into a mask—I was starting to feel pretty lightheaded—and started planning my rebellion.

If the Originem won't hear my complaints, maybe someone else will. Or maybe I am screaming into the void. At this moment, though, I really don't care as I step back to admire my work.

A life-size woman stands before me on the wall, my height and general figure. I've captured her from the side, so we see only the sharp angle of her nose, the downturn of half of her mouth, one wrinkled eye. Her hand is extended in front of her, reaching for objects I've painted just out of reach. Brushes, pencils, a palette—all float beyond her fingertips. It's not a subtle message. It's honestly much more direct than my usual style.

I was limited, though, to four colors with jerry-rigged nozzles, the subdued lighting of the halls at night, and time, being that I am probably not supposed to be doing this. I'm pleased, overall, though, with my work. The woman's face, even from the side-view, is raw and hungry. Her limbs are evidence of her emaciated form, her fingers curling in desperation.

I consider leaving my signature, but even I'm not that stupid. I bundle up all the evidence in the baggy jumpsuit I was issued and turn to leave, but at the last second, I pull out one of the cans—a rusty red—and scrawl under the floating brushes: No art! No life!

It's crude and heavy handed, but it's something. Under the dim lights of the "sleep cycle" I make my way home, my smile never fading.

2

Meshi

I always like going on night runs. I don't mind being on call to help maintenance departments in other divisions, but Khur often jumps on the service calls before I get a chance. He's distracted by his new little human now, though, so when my tablet goes off with a buzz and a red light, I pull my modified jumpsuit over my wings and slip out the door, quietly so I don't wake my mother and brothers.

It's strange and funny to see my sharp-edged friend soften so quickly to one of the new human residents. I've known Khur for years, and he's never exactly been the kind of guy who made small talk in the office. Frankly, he isn't a friendly guy, but he is a good guy. He looked out for my brothers and I when we first arrived here and we've had each others' backs ever since.

We never ate lunch together before today, though. Neither of us could bear to leave while Josep told us everything he knew about these new human women. Khur was rapt because he's determined to make himself a match with Destiny. I couldn't help but listen because it was so *strange*. Flowers and dancing? It actually reminded me of Winged-One's courting rituals a bit. I could appreciate the romance.

It's certainly better than the Dhugaren's wrestle-them-into-submission methods.

I ponder our conversation on women as I walk through the corridors towards the elevator. The lights have already dimmed and the foot traffic is minimal, so when I get to the elevator bay, I am the only one around to take one of the cars up to Division 12.

I quickly find myself in the utility room for one of the subdivisions up here, a community hub for Silfans. Apparently, everyone's nutritional printer is serving brown goo for dinner. Jerrol, the mechanic who usually manages service calls in this division, broke his ankle last week, so it's up to me to make sure everyone here gets dinner. That's a big responsibility.

I better get to work.

Thirty minutes later, I'm leaving the utility room, covered in dust and grime. My head is sore from the bump I got trying to unscrew a particularly stubborn panel and I smell a bit like the raw ingredients that go into the nutritional printers, but everyone in this subdivision is making a less brown and gooey meal to enjoy. Even still, it's a little harder than usual to enjoy my walk back through the dark corridors.

Perhaps this is why, when I hear a strange sound, like a hissing pipe, I raise my eyes to the ceiling, muttering a curse before turning quickly down the next hallway to investigate. I very much want to return to my own division and the warm bed I recently vacated, but I can't ignore a potential safety issue. The citizens of Sanctuary Station depend on us to keep the station safe and running smoothly. I will never be able to go home and sleep knowing there is a potential hazard I ignored. My wings still droop glumly as I follow the sound around another blind corner. And stop in my tracks.

Before me is a sight so beautiful, so perfect, that I nearly drop to my knees in awe. A human woman is standing across the wide corridor, her back to me. She hasn't noticed me yet, so I slink into the shadows to observe her more closely. She's a short thing, but her wild dome of shoulder-length hair seems to give her a few inches. The unruly black curls look soft and sweet-smelling and I suddenly recall Josep telling us about how humans like physical affection. Would she like it if I ran my claws through those luscious curls?

On the ground around her are aerosol cans. I recognize one as an industrial cleaner, but the others have Silfan writing that isn't familiar to me. From what I can tell, she's using the different cans to spray a picture onto the metal wall of the corridor in front of her. It's ingenious, I realize, as I watch her use different chemical reactions to obtain certain colors and affects. The life-size mural comes to life as she works, until eventually she steps back and we both admire her work.

There's so much longing and hunger depicted in the human female drawn on the wall. She looks similar to her artist, but her cheeks are emaciated, her hair limp. Barely out of her reach is a collection of crude art-making tools, some I recognize and some I don't. Physical art is strongly frowned upon by the Originem, though they seemed to make exceptions all the time. For example, Dhugaren weaving is considered 'useful' and therefore acceptable.

I've never felt strongly about it either way before, but now I'm ready to go to Josep and demand paint and brushes so I can give them to this human female. I get a thrill imagining what she could do with real art supplies.

When the lights start to brighten, we both realize we've been standing here all night. I hear her gasp and watch her rush to clean up her mess. I don't want her to see me yet, so I slip back around the corner I came from, sticking to the shadows.

Josep and Khur talked about wooing human women today and I thought the entire ordeal sounded ridiculous at the time. Now, though, I'm considering flowers and dancing in a brand new light. Khur thinks I rush in like a fool, but that's not true. Not when it's something I really want. I can be patient, when I know the reward will be worth it.

3

Hope

I must have just fallen asleep when a pounding sound jolts me awake. It takes me a moment to realize, but then the sound comes again and I realize... it must be the cops.

Oh fuck. I knew this place was going to be a dystopian nightmare. I never should have pushed the boundaries here. Now I'm going to be tossed into space and Prue is going to have to navigate this suspicious sanctuary all by herself.

It's the thoughts of my sister that make me jump out of bed. I don't want to drag her into my mess...again. So I tug my standard-issue jumpsuit over my sleep shorts and speed to the door.

Wait, do I smell like chemicals? I am so, so fucked.

My visitor bangs again as I approach the door and wave my wrist over the panel. The door slides into the wall with a hiss, revealing a tall, grim-faced Originem with his hand still raised to knock. He's so tall the top of his head is hidden above the door jam. Behind his slender frame, I can barely see a Silfan woman with her fists on her hips. She's comically short next to her partner, but her scowl tells me she is the "bad cop" in this scenario.

"Hello, Hope. May we come in?" the Originem asks, throwing me off using my first name in that kind, cautious tone.

Dammit, I was expecting the bad cop first. I wasn't prepared for niceness, especially coming from the much scarier looking of the two. I square my shoulders, giving them my best "come back with a warrant" face.

"Is there something I can help you with, officers?" I ask, trying to keep the sass out of my tone. I really don't want to go to space jail.

"Oh, we're not officers. We are part of the community watch group on division twelve," the Originem says, like that's supposed to make me feel any better. Now I'm picturing aliens with pitchforks.

"I'm Lokas," he continues, "this is Harrow. May we come in?"

He gestures past me with one of those long, double-jointed arms, before ducking his head under the door frame and stepping into my living room, forcing me to either step back or get stepped on. As he crosses the doorway, he seems to unfold, standing a good meter taller than me. The two knee-joints of their long legs only add to the image I have of the Originem creeping through the woods at night to scare campers, like some old Earth cryptid. Behind him, the Silfan walks in and I spare her only a glance. She scoffs audibly, but I'm no fool. I know who the real threat here is.

I should probably feel guilty thinking that. It's ridiculous, really. I should be used to them by now. The Originem saved all of our asses, for crying out loud—but I can't stop the frisson of fear I feel every time I see one. None of the other aliens bother me. Hell, I'm already used to seeing all the different species after three days on the station. Our supposed galactic ancestors, though? There is something about them that freaks me out.

The three of us settle into the standard-issue, sunk-in sectional—all grey, of course—and I rest my elbows on my knees to stop them from bouncing. Across from me, Lokas are Harrow side-by-side and in the back of my mind I realize how comical they would appear sitting together on my couch in literally *any* other situation. Their size difference and the juxtaposition between their expressions as they look back at me is great. I want to draw their caricatures. Prue and I spent a summer drawing them for tourists in Wrigley Market. I wish she were here to see it with me, even though I'm glad I didn't drag her into this mess.

That summer didn't end so well, either, now that I'm thinking about it. I recall drawing a particularly unflattering caricature for a local politician. It's not my fault they didn't know how to take a joke. At least then I had Prue with me.

Now it's just lonely old me facing down an Originem who is looking at me with pity and a Silfan who is looking at me like she wants to bite my head off. Before I can decide which one it's safer to address, Harrow jumps up and points one pastel pink finger at me accusingly.

"We know what you did, so don't try to lie to us," she snarls.

"Hey, now, Harrow. We agreed to be understanding," Lokas says, his voice soft and calm as he turns his attention from his fuming partner to me. "We just have a few questions about your whereabouts last sleep cycle."

"And don't try to lie to us," Harrow snarls again.

"I...uhh..." I'm getting whip-lash from their rapid-fire good cop/bad cop routine.

"Do you even know how hard it is to hand-pick *dersials* off of flower stalks? Not only did you waste good gardening supplies on your vandalism but you *threw the rest away!*" Harrow is really worked up, her pastel pink face darkening to magenta as she yells at me.

"We agreed we wouldn't use negative words like that," Lokas says, sounding so much like an admonishing grandfather it throws me even more off guard.

"Gardening supplies?" I ask dumbly. I feel like they're talking another language. What's a *dersial*?

"Yes, you raided one of the supply closets for the Meadows. What did you expect?" Harrow rolls her eyes like I'm a complete idiot. "Now the volunteers tomorrow are going to have to hand pick all the dersials or they'll overeat the flowers."

I didn't realize they were gardening supplies. I mean...there were also shovels and pots in there, but I thought it was like... a general utility closet. I almost feel bad for the gardeners, especially because I have no clue what *dersials* are.

"We thought we would let you know that tomorrow, the volunteer gardeners meet at 7th hour in front of the Meadows to get started. We hope that you'll be there with them." Lokas says it all very calmly, but I get the feeling that I am very much being volun-*told*.

4

Hope

They don't stick around long once they've doled out my punishment. Harrow departs with a threat to my non-existent balls if I don't show up tomorrow morning. If I weren't so worried, I would be laughing at the fact that balls are weak, vulnerable things in all species. Further proof that females are the better sex, no matter what language we argue in. I don't even question the fact that she thinks I have balls. Maybe all the Silfans do. Or maybe all humans look alike to her and she thinks I'm a man. Ha!

It's a good thing I swore off men ages ago. Not like I'd be beating them off with a stick anyways. I haven't seen a single human man since we left the satellite station last week. When I pointed it out at the landing dock, Prue pointed at one middle aged dude who looked clinically depressed. Like *he* was supposed to single-handedly keep hundreds of women satisfied. Yeah...Okay.

I don't know why my mind drifts this way. It's probably because of how long it's been since I got laid. I swore off sex a few weeks before the world ended, and I haven't broken my vow yet. Slim pickings, you know? My horniness is getting a little harder to ignore though, and well… no human men.

I wouldn't say no to some alien dick, except I'm pretty sure it's taboo here. There's like twenty different kinds of aliens on this space station and I haven't seen one interspecies couple. I read alien smut like it was going out of style my eighteenth summer before I discovered mothman smut. Now that guy can get it. It's something about the wings…but it doesn't seem worth it to draw the attention of the creepy Originem who run this place. Art, on the other hand, is a very different story.

I still haven't moved from my spot on the couch, daydreaming about cryptids and trying to figure out how to get out of my community service tomorrow, when Prue floats through the door. Her long black hair, normally as straight as mine is curly, is a sexually charged rats nest atop her head and a dopey smile graces her angular face. We both got our mother's sharp features, but Prue's harsh lines are softened by her unfamiliar expression. A wary, uncomfortable feeling starts to form in my gut as she sits on the couch Harrow and Lokas recently vacated.

"Have you been gone all night?" I snap, not bothering to temper my tone.

Prue's face immediately falls and the feeling in my gut grows.

"Yes, I have, actually." She sniffs, holding my glare. "I had the most amazing 24-hours, discovered so many incredible places…and people."

"Oh. My. God. You got laid. I have been worried sick, and you were out getting laid," I screech, ignoring the fact that I didn't even know she was missing. I *would* have been worried sick, if I'd known she wasn't here.

"Don't give me that shit, Hope. You probably didn't even realize I was gone," she snaps back. "You've been too wrapped up in your own shit to notice anyone else."

"That's not fair, Prue. You know how important art is to me." I can't believe she would call my very serious concerns *shit*, like I'm just making up drama. I would never do that.

"Give it a rest. They gave you a free tablet for digital art. Have you even opened it?"

"You know technology hates me!" I sputter.

"That's an excuse and you know it." She rolls her eyes and starts picking at the skin around her thumbnails. It's a bad habit she had when we were in high school, but I thought she'd knocked it ages ago.

"Quit picking," I tell her automatically, earning me a scathing look.

"Quit telling me what to do. I'm going to have a life here. My own life. You'll have to find a new sidekick," she tells me, moving to stand.

"Wait!" I shout, ignoring her *sidekick* comment. She's obviously in a mood. "Where were you? Seriously, I really needed you last night."

"I told you, Hope. I was out exploring. I wanted to visit some of the biomes."

"Well, that's lucky, actually," I tell her, "because I got assigned community service at the Meadows and I could really use your company."

"Are you kidding me? We've been here less than a week and you somehow got into trouble already?" Prue rises to her feet, her anger expanding to fill the room. "Well, I won't bail you out this time. You need to fix this by yourself. Leave me out of it."

"Prue, you can't be serious. What if they kick me out?" I ask her, subtly reminding her of what we promised: we'd stick together, no matter what.

When she levels me with an expression of heavy gravity, her next words punch me in the gut. "If you get yourself kicked out, I won't be going with you. We found a home here, Hope. Don't ruin it for yourself, because I'm not letting you ruin it for me."

My chin literally drops, I'm so shocked. My jaw hangs there uselessly as Prue squares her stiff shoulders and walks towards the bedrooms. Pressure builds behind my eyes as I listen to the susurrus of her door opening and closing. Pressing my palms to my eye sockets I resist the urge to scream, instead counting backwards from ten until the pressure abates somewhat.

Shock and betrayal are like lightening bolts burning my insides. A part of me considers doing exactly what she expects and getting kicked off this stupid experimental space station, but that level of self sabotage is beyond even my own craziness. I'm going to have to suck it up and report for community service, all by myself.

"Thanks for volunteering to help. We've got a lot of work to do today."

The Silfan standing in front of the small crowd that's amassed may be all of three feet tall and the color of pink lemonade, but Bazzel is commanding our attention with no problem. I feel a twinge of guilt when she reminds me of the extra work I've caused and all the aliens around me nod eagerly, like they're thrilled to do manual labor for free, all to fix someone else's fuck-ups. Do they know I'm the reason there's a lot to do today? I can feel sweat break out on the back of my neck as I covertly check those closest to me for bad vibes.

I'm so worried about watching out for sneers or toes to the shin, I miss most of what Bazzel instructed and now everyone is getting their own rough-woven sack that is for who knows what?

"I...er.. thank you," I say to Bazzel when she passes me my own sack. She doesn't smile at me sympathetically, just nods, all business, and for some reason that gives me a little strength.

"Wait! Can you... I'm sorry, I missed some of those instructions. Can you go over them again for me?" I ask, cringing.

"You're Hope, right? Thank you for coming to help," she says, appraising me with a fuchsia eye. Silfan pupils are tiny black pinpricks in their oversized eyes and hers are both assessing me coolly.

"I didn't have much of a choice," I mutter.

"Yeah...my mom told me what happened. You're lucky all of those chemicals were non-toxic. They have to be so we can harvest the *dersials* for their meat." She gestures out at the fields of flowers rolling through the meadows for what seems like miles. Above the fields, hundreds of huge bugs dance from bloom to bloom.

They look a bit like golf ball sized cicadas, but function much like bees, from what I gathered in the little I was listening to in her speech. What I didn't hear was...

"Meat?" I say, choking back a gag.

"Yup! I know, I know. Pretty much all the other species react the same way. Silfans are the only obligate carnivores, though, so everyone gets over it pretty quickly when they realize we've got the only real thing in this corner of the galaxy." Bazzel winks at me. "Besides, *dersials* are good. Super crunchy. You'll like them. And if you can fill two entire bags today, I'll buy you a basket of them when we leave."

"You're on," I reply. I'm stuck here either way, and how hard could two bags really be? Besides, eating bugs is no less freaky than eating printed food at every meal.

"I'll meet you here when we're done. You'll hear a chime when it's time to stop." With that, she leaves me with two empty sacks and not much else.

5

Meshi

"Harrow! How are you? Is Ferrel keeping you running?" I greet my friend's wife with a quick winged bow while she ushers me in with no fanfare. Silfans are a very casual race in that way.

"He's driving me crazy, Meshi, as I'm sure you know. That male can't sit still for two seconds, let alone two weeks." She sounds irritated about it, but I know how much affection she holds for her husband. I was there when she arrived in the medic bay...because he wanted me to finish the job he was working on when he sprained his ankle. Harrow isn't wrong when she implies he's a workaholic. I also believe her when she says she'll cuff him to their bed for two weeks if he doesn't follow the doctor's bed rest orders.

The Silfan in question is currently trying to get off the couch he's been stationed on, one leg stretched out stiffly in front of him and the other doing a terrible job of pushing him up. Harrow's by his side in a second, not to help, but to push him back into the cushions with a force you wouldn't expect of her small frame.

"Quit that right now, you idiot," she hisses, "Meshi came to wish you well, not see you hurt yourself more."

Completely unphased, Ferrel stretches his neck enough to plant a kiss on his wife's cheek before smiling at me sheepishly.

"She takes good care of me, whether I like it or not," he says as I settle in the chair across from him, tucking my wings into my sides awkwardly. Because of the membranes of our wings, my kind can't use "arm" chairs very comfortably.

"I can see that. And it's a good thing, too," I tease him.

"Yes, it's a wonder she puts up with me."

"It's because you listen to all my grumbling," she tells him from her perch on the armrest behind him, reaching down to fluff his pillow. "I was just telling him about my morning visit on behalf of the community watch."

The furniture is made to fit the residents of the apartment, so she can comfortably rest one of her petite feet on the ground while she speaks, while I am squeezed into the armchair, knees-to-chest, like a family of *battran* hanging from the eaves, all squished together for warmth. I don't mind, though. Seeing them being all domestic and nurturing is doing twisty things to my insides. Would my artist fluff her spouse's pillow? Worry over them when they're injured? I may not have spoken to her—dont even know her name!—but I feel like I know her. She is full of passion and fire. I bet when she loves someone, she does it with her whole self.

I'm so preoccupied in my daydream I don't hear what Harrow is saying for a minute.

"...the thing is, I actually like the art, and I think I understand what she's trying to say. The Originem certainly don't foster a lot of artistic freedom here, for all they talk about uto—"

"Wait, wait, go back. You met my artist?" I blurt out when her words start to register again.

"Your artist?" She asks with the quirk of one of her coral eyebrows.

"Well, what I mean is...I saw her. It. I saw the mural yesterday after I fixed the nutritional printers," I recover lamely.

"Hmm. Yesterday during the sleep-cycle, right? That's when you finished the job?" Harrow asks, leaning towards me slightly.

"Rein in the detective, honey," Ferrel says affectionately, patting his partner's leg.

"I'm just saying, that's when Hope was *making* the mural. So..." She leaves the sentence hanging there, smiling at me smugly, and I chuckle at her forcefulness.

Harrow was a detective before she left their home planet, a fact their daughter, Bazzel, hated growing up. Experiencing the piercing gaze of her inquisition, I can see why. She probably didn't get away with anything. Harrow seems to soften before my eyes, though.

"She's got a heavy load on her back, that one," she muses.

"I'm not sure what that means," I admit.

"It's a Silfan phrase... like, she's carrying the weight of all her life's burdens," Ferrel explains.

"I think maybe someone like you would be good for her," Harrow says, with a fond look at her spouse, "She reminded me a lot of me, when I was a bit younger. So full of fire, I needed someone who was as smooth and calm as water."

I sputter and my wing-joints hit the arms of my chair-cage in surprise. "You think I'm calm and smooth as water?" I ask incredulously.

"Well...maybe not. I suppose if we are considering the traditional Silfan elemental divination aspects, I would consider you to be air, wouldn't you agree, dear?" Ferrel says, quirking his neck up at Harrow.

"Oh, completely. Light, fun, a little playful, but also very tranquil and serene at times. Maybe a good match for our little artist. We're going to have to keep an eye on her, anyways. Can't have her getting into too much trouble," she sighs deeply, like the whole thing is exhausting her. I know Harrow, though, and she's going to end up adopting Hope like she has the rest of this station's strays. "Besides, I sent her to the Meadows to volunteer with Bazzel as punishment, and I'm positive *and* positively terrified that the two of them are going to hit it off immediately."

"She's at the Meadows? Right now?" I jump up, not even bothering to hide my enthusiasm. Harrow's right, I am air. I feel like it right now as I bounce towards their door, eager to actually meet the girl of my daydreams. "So sorry, I must be off. Glad to see you're resting up, Ferrel. Don't hesitate to buzz our team if you need anything done while you're down. Harrow, always a pleasure. Bye!"

I barely hear their responses as I bound out the door, remembering not a moment too soon that the ceilings in this division aren't tall enough to fly down the hallways here. Cursing, I take off at an awkward jog. My body isn't made for speedy land travel, but sky above, I am not going to let this opportunity pass me by.

By the time I arrive at the Silfan biome, I can feel sweat beading in between the folds of my wings. I'm sure my bald head looks especially shiny under this artificial sunlight. I can't introduce myself like this. Josep said first impressions are important to humans. Pulling my handkerchief from my back pocket, I try to clean myself up as I make my way towards the tall, grassy meadows. The rolling fields go on past my sight line, each one brimming with colorful flowers.

I can see citizens dotted throughout the fields, but no matter how I squint I don't recognize the tiny figure of a human woman amongst them. Nothing for it but to get closer, I guess. I almost take flight, but decide to stay on the ground. Don't want to frighten her off before she's gotten to know me.

Besides, the Meadows are beautiful from any angle. Admittedly, nothing beats an aerial view. I'm a Winged-One after all. From the sky, though, I wouldn't be able to see the detailed inner workings of the complex Silfan flowers spread out before me. The vermillion blooms dominating one of the further fields are probably my favorite, their amber-colored stamens oversized and showy. On instinct, I head in that direction.

I find her in that exact field, surrounded by my favorite flowers, and I'm no fool to overlook a sign from fate. Her thick black hair is the only thing that I see among the wash of delightful, bright orange blossoms. She's so tiny she could be a flower herself, with her unruly curls making my new favorite petals. She's focused on her task, not noticing me making my way closer to her. Her face comes into view between the waving stalks of flowers and I hesitate, crouching a bit to hide myself behind the foliage.

Now is perhaps not the best time to introduce myself. Hope's face is red, her eyes and nose scrunched up to make adorable ridges between her brows—only they're not supposed to be adorable, because she doesn't have the ridged brow that my people do. I'm pretty sure that expression is one of anger. She moves among the tall stalks and I almost moan at the sight revealed to me. She's stripped down the top half of her jumpsuit and tied the sleeves around her waist. Her pale skin is glistening with sweat, the tiny, form-fitting, grey shirt she's wearing that only covers a band of skin across her chest, is dark with moisture and even from my post several yards away, creeping in the flowers stalks, I can see the peaked outline of her nipples.

She quickly disappears from view, stomping noisily and dragging a half full sack behind her that's leaving a slimy trail. With my sensitive hearing, I can hear her muttered curses as she moves away from me. She's going to be even more furious when she learns that all those *dersials* she harvested are worthless. The crunchy insects are fried whole. Once their squishy inner bodies spill out, they are no longer edible.

Should I tell her that? Do I want to be the giver of bad news during our first interaction? That doesn't seem like a good first impression at all. Maybe I could offer to help her harvest?

Only, I don't want her to think I see her as weak, or in need of help. It's all in the approach, though. I believe coming to her rescue could be a great first impression. I've made my mind up to step out of my hiding spot and reveal myself when the chime signaling the end of the day sounds. I've volunteered here a few times with my brother, Maklash and I know they'll gather near the entrance to unload their cargo. Hope is going to have to turn around and walk right past me to leave. Without thinking, I jump to my left, concealing myself in a particularly thick bushel of foliage.

"Hello? Who's there?" Hope calls out, "Bazzel, I swear to fuck if you're pranking me, I'm going to beat you with this sack of bugs!"

There's no fear in her voice, just fire, and I'm struck again with the conviction that I need this woman in my life. Her passionate attitude lights something up inside of me that I'm not even sure existed before. As she walks away, grumbling and cursing the whole time, a strange contentment settles over me. Because in the foliage I've landed in, hell all over this field, *dersials* are still buzzing about, way too thickly populated for healthy fields. That means they'll be harvesting again tomorrow. I know just how I am going to introduce myself to Hope.

6

Hope

Harvesting *dersials* is miserable work. They look a bit like cicadas, but they're as big as golf balls, and they're *fast* when they want to be, darting away from my outstretched hand every time I reach for one. I thought it would be easy, seeing them climbing the thick stalks of the flowers in my assigned field and buzzing around the oversized, bright yellow-orange stamens. I love a challenge, and in truth, I do feel a little guilty about causing this whole situation, but—fuck—this was too much.

Yesterday, it took the entire day to get maybe a dozen of the stupid things, mostly by squishing them or stomping. I'd stripped down to my sports bra by midday and sweated more than I have in years. I brought my squishy, half-empty, singular bag to Bazzel and she had a good laugh at my expense explaining that I need to lull the bugs first, with sound or smoke, then I can pluck them off the ground like stones.

Apparently, that's the information I missed while I was having a moment yesterday afternoon. Also, *obviously* (Bazzel said, like this should be common knowledge), the *dersials* have to be harvested whole. Once they're squished they're contaminated—inedible. Then she gave me a really old looking carved wooden instrument that reminds me of those animal guiros we used to get at the flea market and said that it would help me next time, like she knew I was going to show up today again when she announced there was more work to be done.

I wasn't going to. I was only volun-told about the one day. The instrument sat heavy in my jumpsuit pocket, though, when I pulled it on this morning. I had to admire Bazzel's underhanded tactics with the *dersials* yesterday. I probably even deserved it since I was the one who caused all the extra work to begin with. I could appreciate the subtle viciousness behind her prank. What really rankled me was her kindness, though. Giving me the *falofon* and walking me through its purpose, with no snide remark about why this conversation was necessary to begin with. When she told the group they'd meet again today, she didn't even glance my way. That irked me.

She should have sneered at me. Really made me feel the weight of the guilt, pressured me into coming back to fix my mess. That's what I would have done. Instead she said, "thanks for coming out," and waved me off with a polite smile.

What kind of game is she playing? I've been pondering it all morning. I would have asked Prue what she thought, but she was gone again when I woke up. Her words eat at me, too. She demanded that I *fix* this. I guess that's what I have to do.

Which is why at the fourteenth hour of this weird twenty five hour cycle I find myself standing once again with a small gathering of volunteers, listening intently this time for Bazzel's instructions. Most of the volunteers are Silfan again, but there's also a Winged-One standing on the edge of the crowd.

The weird wings-for-arms thing does something strange to me, and I study the solid, sinewy lines that make perfect geometry of his alien limbs until his head cocks towards me, those huge bat-like ears seeming to point in my direction. My eyes swivel forward and rivet to Bazzel, my face in flames as I realize I once again missed the last part of her instructions.

With a frustrated huff I stomp towards the bright yellow field I was working in yesterday as the other citizens do the same. I keep my eyes firmly ahead, refusing to check which field the Winged-One went to. The last thing I need is a weirdly hot alien distraction to soften me to this place. I still haven't seen any mixed couples here. Maybe they're taboo. I wouldn't be surprised, with the creepy Originem overlords they have running the place.

I'm going to have to have a word with Prue. She was definitely dickmatized this morning. Or cuntmatized? Is that a word? Puss-merized? I'd love to ask my sister, but she's still mad at me.

At first the funny little instrument doesn't help at all and I think it must be another one of Bazzel's pranks, but eventually I get the hang of it and the *dersials* start dropping like stones. It becomes much easier—and much more rewarding—work after that.

I still have a mission. I still miss art like breathing, but there's not much I can do about it now and to my surprise, keeping my hands busy keeps my mind off of it in a nice way. It also helps that the vibrant colors of the rolling fields of flowers feed something in my soul.

I'm back in the golden yellow field, like mutated daffodils, these flowers bob and wave at me. And the smell! They're so sweet and floral, it's amazing.

The *dersials* themselves have opalescent wings, like fat, flamboyant dragonflies. I wonder if they cook the wings or remove them. If I crush a whole bunch of them up and mix them with some kind of clear sealant I could make the prettiest glaze.

At the end of the day, I have two full bags of *dersials* buzzing quietly in my bag and Bazzel's wide eyes make me think she perhaps didn't expect me to take to the wooden instrument so quickly.

"Still gonna treat me to some of these things deep fried?" I ask smugly. After an entire two days harvesting I'm weirdly desensitized to the concept of eating bugs and I'm also fucking starving.

"Sure. Here, take our bags over to the drop off site and I'll go get our snacks," she hands me two buzzing bags and heads towards the exit with a wave.

The Silfans have everything very organized. There's a neat, orderly line of citizens waiting to drop their harvest off at the long table they have set up under a spacious gazebo, like the kind people would get married in back on Earth. A few Silfans and a lone Originem stand on the other side of the table, someone taking the bags and weighing them, another jotting down notes, then the Originem takes the bag and puts it in a stainless steel freezer that's as tall as he is. It's a very efficient process and I'm quickly to the front of the line.

"Hope, I'm glad to see you out here today." Now that I'm closer, I see that the Silfan woman taking the bags and weighing them is Harrow. My guard immediately goes up. Only forty eight hours ago she was playing bad cop in my living room and now she's smiling at me with genuine affection? I don't trust it.

"Uh...thanks?"

She lifts one of those judgy, coral eyebrows, but keeps her lips pursed as she takes all four bags from me.

"Four bags on your second day? You must be a natural gardener," she says after balancing the bags in the metal basin plate of the industrial size scale.

"Only two are mine. The other two are Bazzel's."

"Oh, you met my daughter? Good, I thought you two might get on well," she tells me, then turns to the soft blue Silfan taking notes and lists off a few measurements I don't recognize.

"Bazzel is your daughter?" I thought she might have mentioned that yesterday, but there was a lot going on. I can see the resemblance. They're both tiny, bossy terrors.

"My one and only. My stubborn girl," she says fondly.

The sweet, wry expression she gets transforms her face. In this moment, she reminds me of my mother, whose love was sarcastic and dry, but no less fierce because of it. This is exactly something my mom would do, forcing someone to do community service so she could play friend-maker for her daughter. I'm just glad she doesn't have a son. My throat feels a little tight as I swallow the memories down. Both of my parents died in the initial disasters on Earth. I miss them every day, but having Prue makes it easier. When we're fighting, it's like all my weak spots are exposed and the world keeps pressing on the purple and green bruises showing up.

"She's actually gone to get us some *dersials*, so I better go. Don't want her waiting on me," I choke out, then I skedaddle away from the gazebo like my pants are on fire.

I catch Bazzel as she's walking back into the biome, her hands full and her hot pink hair gleaming under the artificial sunlight. She smiles when she sees me and I have to admit that having a friend again, or maybe the beginnings of one, feels nice. The weight of the world is a little bit lighter than it was a moment ago. I smile back, reaching for the basket of golden, grease-shiny, hush puppy looking things she's handing me.

"They usually have salty and spicy varieties. You seem like a more spicy kind of female," she tells me. "But I have the salty ones here if you want to try them."

"No this is perfect," I moan around a bite of crunchy, spicy goodness. They continue to remind of hush puppies, except they're way crunchier, with a slightly chewy center. The flavor is somewhat like spicy buffalo sauce, and altogether the *dersials* could almost pass for popcorn chicken, or boneless wings.

"I could totally get used to eating bugs," I tell Bazzel, swiping one of the salty ones from her basket as we sit in a field of short grass.

"See! I don't know why so many people freak out about it," she says, stretching her legs out in front of her with a sigh.

"I think it's the visual, you know? The legs and the...pincers?"

"Ha, yeah I guess I could see that."

"It is kind of weird, seeing them flying around out there while we're eating their friends," I say, chuckling.

"Nah, I do it to establish dominance," Bazzel tells me, looking at me with a gleam in her eye.

"What does that even mean?" I snort.

"I get fried *dersials* after every harvest, come in here and eat them in front of the survivors," she says, "Like I said, establishes dominance. Plus, it makes me feel better about spending a whole day, now two, picking the little assholes off the flower stems."

"That is the most ridiculous thing I've ever heard," I say, unable to hold back my laughter. My palms sink into the cool, soft earth as I lean on my hands and laugh. It feels so good to let go for a moment, and when I hear Bazzel snort-laughing next to me, I start back up all over again.

After my giggles finally subside, I ask the other question that has been on my mind today.

"What's up with this field? I saw a few others, too. No flowers, the grass is short. Did they die or something?"

"Die? Oh, no. Just means they were up for rotation. When a field becomes mature, we harvest the flowers for the wind riders and let the field lie fallow for a while before planting again."

"What's a wind rider?" I ask.

Bazzel's fuchsia eyes get wide and adorable, like she's about to get a present.

"Have you not heard of the Silfan Wind Riders yet? We're awesome. You should come check us out tomorrow."

"Ok! Is it like hang gliding? I used to do that back home," I tell her. I'm already dreaming of sweeping landscapes, ethereal horizons. I miss hang gliding. I didn't think I'd ever be able to do it again. Biome or not, I'm sure the view of the meadows from above are breathtaking.

"Maybe. I don't know what that is," she quips. "There's spare flyers if you wanna give it a go, though."

"Uhh just, give it a go?" My voice rises a few octaves. "Seems slapdash."

Bazzel shrugs carelessly, popping her last *dersial* in her mouth and chomping down with her pointy white fangs. "You can see if they look like your hang riders. They are stored in the garage next to the entrance."

"Hang gliders," I correct her absentmindedly. It's been a while, but I think I could probably pick up hang gliding again pretty quickly. This "wind-riding" can't be too much different. And what else am I doing with my time? There's no paint or brushes to be found, my sister has effectively abandoned me for the natives, and I can barely navigate the corridors here. Getting to the Meadows was a feat of sheer determination.

"Whatever," Bazzel responds. " I'll give you a tutorial before we take off. Only if you want to. We meet weekly. You can always watch this week and fly another time, if you're scared." I swear there is a taunt laced into her tone, her narrowed eyes.

Indignation shoots through my spine, making it stiffen.

"Humans usually think those words are mocking... like a challenge," I tell Bazzel stiffly. She's alien after all and maybe didn't mean them that way.

Bazzel raises one fuschia eyebrow at me, gaze full of dares.

"Silfans think the same."

"Well, I'm certainly not scared of flying. I was born for it," I tell her haughtily, dusting off my crumby hands in the grass and rising to my feet.

Bazzel follows me towards the entrance, showing me where to recycle my snack basket by the garage where the wind riders are stored. They're similar to hang gliders in shape and function, though the single control bar is replaced by two long handlebars like on a beach cruiser bicycle. They're also a bit smaller than hang gliders from Earth, which makes sense, but luckily I'm on the small side for a human, myself.

"I think I can fly one of these things," I tell Bazzel excitedly.

"Great, meet me here tomorrow afternoon, then." With a wave she takes off, but I stay for a while longer, my heart fuller than it has been in a year now, staring at the colorful Silfan Wind Riders lined up in the garage.

7

Meshi

I was going to introduce myself today, see if perhaps Hope wanted to harvest a field together. During Bazzel's little introduction, though, she kept glancing at me. Her dark eyes would touch me and then skate away as soon as I met them with my own. She's as flighty as a young *battran*, which surprises me. She seemed so fiery, so confident when I saw her before. That's part of what drew me to her. Hope has seemed up to this point like someone who would not scare easily.

I find myself hesitating, now. Not because I'm no longer interested, but because I worry that I might scare her off. There aren't any interspecies couples here, yet, but I genuinely don't think it would be a problem. I've lived here since I was a baby and I've never known anything but love and acceptance. The humans only just got here, though. Hope couldn't know what to expect about life on Sanctuary Station, even if she watched the orientation videos a hundred times.

When Bazzel claps her hands and shoos everyone off to start harvesting *dersials*, I fall back into the shadows of the few trees that dot the borders of different meadows. Hope heads to the amber fields again, carrying a Silfan *falofon*, an instrument mainly given to Silfan children to distract them. It's a wooden oval from their home planet with different patterns of grooves and knobs carved into it. A dowel pierces through the middle and can be pulled out and rubbed against the oval to produce different sounds. I think it may be hollow inside, I am not certain.

What I am certain of is that the *falofon* is not going to help her catch *dersials.* Perhaps a seasoned player might be able to eke out the low note required to mesmerize the bugs, but it was difficult. All the other volunteers had their datapads tucked into their jumpsuits, tuned to the frequency required, but Hope seemed to have missed those instructions. And also left her datapad at home. Should I offer my services? I don't even need technology to make these bugs drop like ripe fruit. I see little clouds of dust puffing up from each of her steps as she stomps down the last few yards of path towards her chosen field. Perhaps she would not be amenable to assistance right now.

Instead, I crouch low, keeping out of Hope's sight, even easier to do once she is in the field and dwarfed by the big blooms, and follow her into the thick of it. When she starts clumsily tapping on the *falofon* with the dowel, I almost groan out loud. It's an agonizing minute before she switches to rubbing the dowel across the different textures. She makes a delightful noise of joy at her small success and starts working on her technique, turning the oval in one hand and scraping the dowel at different speeds, watching the *dersials* that bob and weave harmlessly through the air from bud to bud.

She may not be able to lull a bug, but a Winged-One is a different matter entirely. I almost forget why I'm here, I'm so mesmerized by the way she sticks her tongue out of the corner of her mouth when she's concentrating hard on something. I'm enthralled by her unruly, uncontrollable halo of black hair that gets constantly in her face and how, occasionally, she'll blow it up off her forehead in a loud, gusty breath, only for it to float back down again.

The next loud, gusty breath sounds much more exasperated, though, and my brain boots back online. What am I doing? Am I really hiding here, watching her, like a complete creep? Well, I certainly can't introduce myself now. Should I leave? I could easily slip out of here unheard by her, but there are other citizens around. If Bazzel sees me, she'll tell her parents, and I'll never hear the end of it. They'll probably have to start some sick new kind of rehab for people like me, creepy stalkers.

Just a few yards in front of me and completely oblivious, Hope growls adorably, rearing her hand back as if to throw the *falofon* before stopping herself. She brings the instrument up, holding it with both hands inches from her face and starts to whisper-screech to it, to my absolute amazement.

"Now you listen here, you little shit. If you are a prank or something by Bazzel it's gonna be my last mother fucking straw. I am trying to do the right thing here and clean up after my own mistakes, so," she pauses, taking a few deep breaths, "you better start making these bugs drop it like it's fucking hot, or so help me."

She doesn't finish the threat, but she doesn't need to. She's talking to an inanimate object. She's lecturing a children's party toy. She might be absolutely insane, but it's also the cutest thing I've ever seen. When she starts scraping again, I make sure to start humming.

It's a useless artifact of evolution at this point, but I'm sure glad for it now. Winged-Ones from the homeworld used it to navigate dark caves and hunt without light or audible sound. Audible being the key word here, because the low frequency made with my infrasonic echolocation is impossible to hear for most species. And it happens to be the perfect tone for putting *dersials* to sleep.

It's so effective that every bug in this field drops immediately, plopping onto the dirt and grass with little patters, like raindrops. Hope gasps, turning in a circle and I duck down and stop humming, even though I doubt she could hear or see me.

"Holy shit," she mutters as the insects around us start to stir. When she picks her instrument up again, I am ready.

By the time the afternoon bell chimes, I'm sweating and my throat aches, but I'm pleased to see Hope has two full sacks of buzzing *dersials*, waking up from their most recent nap. I consider approaching her, debating whether or not she'd be upset that I deceived her and spied on her, but then Bazzel is dragging her out of the field and towards the harvesting station, and I watch from the shadows of the tall, amber flowers as they leave.

I'm not one to admit defeat, but maybe it's time to admit that there will never be a good time to introduce myself to Hope. If humans value first impressions, maybe I'm not a good match for one. The thought slumps my shoulders, makes my claws feel so heavy my wings could drag the ground.

I've yet to meet a Winged-One who held my attention. My brother Shemo is in love with a Dhugaren woman, but I haven't been interested in any female I've met yet. Until Hope, that is.

I slouch further as I make my way around the large barn that houses the Silfan Wind Riders. Hope would love the wind riders. She's so fearless.

I must be daydreaming especially hard, because for a moment I swear I hear her voice. Making my way around the corner of the barn, I see that one of the wide doors has been pulled open and two figures stand in its shadow.

Ducking back around the corner, I calm my racing heart enough to overhear them.

"I think I can fly one of these things," Hope says to Bazzel.

"Great, meet me here tomorrow afternoon, then," the Silfan replies.

Perking up, I slip back around the barn before Bazzel spots me as she walks away. Hope stays behind with the gliders and I want to go in and talk to her so badly. It's not the right time, though. Instead, I make my way back to my division.

Tomorrow, we'll go flying. Tomorrow will be perfect.

Ma is at the kitchen table, like she always is. When it's just her there, the sturdy furniture provided by the Originem looks so big, even though my brothers and I knock wings every time we're all sitting down for dinner, which is most nights. Shemo is probably somewhere sulking about Furga, but I can hear the musical indication that my other older brother is in our shared room, playing. He's always playing music, whether he's practicing it, writing it, or performing it. He *lives and breathes the melody*, as he's fond of saying.

In the kitchen, Ma sits alone, flipping through a waxy old photo album. The pages crack and crinkle as she turns them with care, tracing a tall, lithe Winged-One's figure in the dim photo in front of her.

"You always remind me of him the most, you know?" She asks, looking up at me with a wistful smile.

It's something I've heard a hundred times before, but I nod like it's still exciting. For me, it is. I'm the youngest and I was still a kit when my dad passed. I can't remember him as well as Shemo and Maklash can. Hearing these stories is the closest I can get to feeling like I really knew him.

"Why's that, Ma?" I ask her, settling into the seat next to her to listen.

"He was so kind. He wanted to help everyone, all the time. When we first got married I was always annoyed at him for missing dinner half the time because he was fixing an oven so someone else wouldn't miss their own dinner. I thought he needed to take care of himself more." She turns the page again, the tip of her claw carefully pinning a picture flat. I already know the one. The resemblance really is uncanny, especially in the nose and brow. "You really are so much like him."

"Hey! I didn't miss dinner tonight. Only once, this whole week, in fact!" I tease her, trying to get a smile out of my melancholy mother. She only looks at me with big, black eyes.

"You need someone to take care of you, Meshi. That's what I realized back home," she always referred to Bejkarr as home, saying that's where we left Dad, so that's where her home will always be. "Your father had to take care of the neighbor-karst. It was his calling, his purpose. He made the world a better place because of it. So I had to step up and take care of him. You need someone to take care of you, my sweet son. You take care of this whole station-karst."

I love how she still uses phrases from Bejkarr, too, even though it annoys my brothers to no end. It makes me feel connected to it in a way that comes naturally to them. They walk through the cavernous Winged-One's biome and they experience nostalgia. I feel like I've forgotten something important and no matter what I do, I can't remember it.

I lean over and kiss the top of my mothers smooth, hairless head, using the table to push myself onto my feet. "I don't need anyone else taking care of me, Mama. You and those two buffoons out there do plenty." Walking over to the nutritional printer, I start fiddling with buttons before turning back around, "Why don't you go put your album up while I make us all some dinner."

Her sigh is long and drawn out, but she nods like I knew she would. "You should really get Maklash to make dinner. He's been holed up with his instruments again all day today."

"It's just pressing a few buttons," I say as I do that. "Tell Maklash to put down the *dopticana* long enough to eat a meal. His wings were practically translucent last time I saw him."

She *tsks*, but does as I say, folding the book closed and sliding it into the middle of the kitchen table, next to a chaotic, geometric sculpture that catches my eye. It's not new, in fact it's one of those things that's been around for so long—all my life, actually—that it blends into the background, right there in the center of the table. I forget it exists most days.

"Wait," I blurt out. "Will you tell me about the statuette again, Ma?"

She looks at me curiously before nodding, turning back to the table to pick up the carved stone. It's an abstract piece, full of hand-carved squares stacked and twisted around, creating windows and stairways that lead to nowhere. It is small enough to hold in your hands, but big enough to get lost in for hours, looking for patterns and tiny details. The stone had been a solid geode, so that around the outermost parts are a flat grey, but inside is a kaleidoscope of pale colors. Pale white quartz mingles with the turquoise and barely-there violet. She holds it up to the light to see through the transparent crystal for a moment before handing it out to me. I take it gingerly.

"Your father made this for me, when we were courting. It was tradition on Bejkarr, you know, for the males to find a crystalline stone and carve a vision of their future into it. Lots of embracing figurines, or carved hearths. Your father knew I would have hated those," she tells me, her voice bittersweet and full of longing. "You already know this story. Why do you ask now?" She asks like she already knows the answer. Behind me, the nutritional printer beeps, letting us know the food is done. We both ignore it.

She's right, of course. I do know this story. I know that the strange, abstract sculpture was one of the reasons she fell for Dad. He was always running around, helping everyone in their community, but he never failed to make her feel seen. The stone carving is an old courting tradition, evolved from long before our people were forced into caves on our home planet, when we used to fly under open skies and carve intricate totems from the wide-trunked trees of Bejkarr.

"Just...curious. I wonder if anyone still does these here?" I walk over and lovingly put the statuette in its place.

"Well, I think Nurl's son made one when he was courting the girl on division sixteen, do you remember? They got married, oh... six months ago maybe?"

"Hm," is all I say, lost in thought. I would guess he got the stone from the Winged-One biome, which is on division sixteen. The Originem probably made sure there was a good stock of geodes for situations like that. They're good about helping its citizens maintain their cultural mating traditions.

"Do you...have someone in mind you would like to carve for?" She ventures timidly.

"Maybe. I'm not sure they would get the significance of the ritual."

Even as I say that, I know I'm wrong. Hope appreciates art and I know this is exactly the kind of thing that will win her heart. The thought makes my own heart pound crazily against my rib cage, excitement already taking over the nerves. I consider waiting to introduce myself until after I make the sculpture, but it will take too long. I can't wait weeks to speak to her, to learn what makes her laugh and what makes her angry, besides collecting *dersials*.

"Ahh, I see. She is not Winged-One." Ma purses her lips in thought.

I know she won't mind that detail. She has been pressuring Shemo to make a move on Furga for ages. She just wants her sons to be happy, she reminds us daily. So I give her a moment to think, turning back to the fresh food that finished printing and doling it onto separate dishes. Then I slide it onto the chrome counter and turn back to Ma. The food can wait for a moment, but this conversation cannot.

"I think that introducing her to some of our courting rituals is a lovely idea," Ma tells me. "But only if you make an effort to learn about hers as well."

"Flowers," I tell her, then explain further at her confused look. "Humans like flowers and dancing and... diamonds, *precious stones.* They gift them to their chosen mates."

It's so fitting and so perfect, how did I not see this before? Ma obviously agrees because she lovingly taps her claws against mine, the click-click sound filling me with affection.

"That, my son, sounds like serendipity."

Then she waltzes out of the room, presumably to get Maklash for dinner, her wings billowing behind her like the folds of a long, luxurious gown.

8

Hope

For the first time in a long time I wake up... excited. I fling the covers off with glee, putting on my boring grey jumpsuit with vigor. I remember the rush of hang-gliding back on Earth, the mixture of thrill and joy and a tinge of fear that made for a heady, unforgettable experience. I can't wait to try it in the Meadows. An aerial view of their rolling flower fields might even beat the pictures I've seen of old Holland, before tulips went extinct. I am bouncing on my toes down the hallway towards the kitchen when the most heavenly scent reaches my nose. The dark, rich aroma of coffee.

Am I still dreaming? Did Prue find a secret code for the nutritional printer that no one told me about? Speedwalking the rest of the way, I find my sister standing at the long, chrome counter next to the nutritional printer stirring two steaming cups of dark liquid. I blatantly ignore the discolored, deteriorating section of the countertop where I did my earlier experiments. Bugspray should *not* have that effect on metal.

"Prue, tell me that's what I think it is," I say, the hope in my voice making it high and fluttery.

She looks at me with a sly smile, holding one of the cups out to me with both hands. "Why don't you try some and find out?"

I take it gingerly, like one might hold a holy relic, and bring the rim to my nose, inhaling deeply. The liquid is dark brown and opaque, like a good strong brew. I blow on the steam rising from the surface for a moment, but I can't wait for it to cool down. I'll burn my tongue for this. It's rich and bitter when it hits my tongue and maybe it's a placebo effect, but I immediately feel a little caffeine boost. It's got a bit of an aftertaste like pistachio that's nutty and creamy. The taste and feel of it is close enough to coffee that I feel an immediate wave of nostalgia. I have to tilt my chin up so the tear that's gathering doesn't fall.

"Prudence Maria Anderson. I love you. I've told you I love you lately, right?" I say, sipping my drink and ignoring my burning tongue.

She chuckles, grabbing her drink and gesturing for me to join her at our small kitchen table, just enough room for two chairs. I slide in across from her and only when we're both seated and facing each other do I remember we're fighting right now. The coffee completely distracted me. I feel my shoulders rise before I can stop them, instantly on the defense. Is she expecting an apology now? Before I can decide whether or not to do it—the coffee is a really good incentive—Prue beats me to it.

"Hope, I'm really sorry about what I said yesterday," she tells me. "I don't want us to ever split up. I just want you to *want* to be here."

I nod, taking another sip. The caffeine convinces me to be nice.

"I do. I do want to be here. I understand we have different priorities right now and that's ok. I wanted to help. I have to look out for you.

You're my sister." Even I can admit that was a shit apology, but I can only be so nice.

"You always seem to forget I'm the older one. If one of us should be looking out for the other, it's obviously me," she says, exasperated.

That's what she always says, but that's not really true. She may be older, but I'm the tough one. Prue's always been the softer of the two of us, the more pliant. She likes to go with the flow and tries not to cause any waves. I don't give a fuck if I make a tsunami if it gets me what I want. Prue says it's because I'm the youngest in the family and everyone spoiled me rotten. I prefer to think I'm a confident, outspoken woman who knows how to get what she wants. I'm trying to keep the peace around here, though, so I don't bother pointing all this out.

"We need to look out for each other," I say placatingly. "Just let me know next time you're not going to be home all night so I don't worry, okay?"

"I can do that." She nods, and we sit together in companionable silence for a minute drinking our coffees. I don't even mind that there's no milk or sugar. After a while, we both drain our cups and toss them in the bottom of the printer for sanitizing. I see a metal canister of dark brown coffee grounds on the counter that I hadn't noticed before.

"You really did find coffee," I exclaim once I've had a moment to enjoy it. "Where? How?"

"Well, actually, I'm glad you asked because I wanted to tell you about a new friend of mine," she says haltingly.

My shoulders go up again and I have to work hard to relax them. I should have known this was going to be related to whoever kept her out all night yesterday. Are the aliens using coffee to seduce people? I'm a total goner if so.

"A *friend*, is it? Or is it a *frieeend*?" I ask, wiggling my eyebrows because I know it will make her mad.

"Well," she starts primly.

I have to physically bite my tongue to stop myself calling her *Prudey Prudence* like I did in high school.

"I don't quite know yet," she continues, "but I know that I would like you to meet her. Her biome is where the *subus* are grown. The coffee beans."

"That's sweet and all, but I'm not sure getting freaky with the locals is a good idea, Prue," I confess.

"Wow, I can't believe *you're* the one being a prude this time," she scoffs at me. "Besides, the orientation videos were pretty clear about how acceptable it was. Encouraged, even."

Well if that don't make every alarm bell in my head start ringing. I set my mug on the table with a loud thud. I didn't watch the videos. I couldn't figure out how to use the datapads. Prue was supposed to tell me the important stuff, but *that* certainly never came up.

"That's fucking weird. Why would they do that?"

She shrugs. "I don't know. It just kind of happened, with me and...Listen, I don't think it's that big of a deal. I want you to meet her. You'll love her, seriously."

I knew this place was too good to be true. They're bribing her with coffee. And sex. Ah, geez. We're all goners. Is this the point where I decide to join them, since I can't beat them? I eye Prue speculatively. She looks happy. Nervous right now, for some reason, but all morning she's had a nice little glow to her that's been good to see. I'm not sure what for yet, but I'm keeping my guard up until I find out. Until then, I have to watch out for my sister.

"I'd love to meet your new friend, Prue. Especially if they have coffee," I tell her, pulling her in for a quick hug before heading back out of the kitchen. "Tell me when and where and I'll be there."

"Thanks, sis. Wait, Where are you going?"

"I'm going hang-gliding in the Meadows. I made a friend, too," I say, stopping in the doorway and turning to look at her. I almost invite her but her comment from the other day sticks with me. If she wants her own life, I have to have my own, too.

There's a flash of hurt on her face, but she quickly covers it with a smile. "Wow, that sounds great! Have fun! Tell me all about it tonight?"

"Of course!" Walking back over, I wrap her into a more forceful hug. She's a few inches taller than me and I have to stand on my tiptoes to tuck my chin over her shoulder. "We'll catch up tonight."

I hate that it feels like we're drifting apart. We've been stuck at the hips since I was born, pretty much. The thought of us growing apart from each other and closer to some strangers, aliens or not, makes me sick to my stomach. Prue may have completely drank the kool-aid here on Sanctuary Station, but I'm not completely sold yet.

The meadow is buzzing, and not with *dersials* this time. There's a sea of Silfans so diverse it's like a pastel rainbow swirling around dozens of gliders, I mean wind riders, they've wheeled out into a wide, bare plateau. I see what Bazzel meant when she said they saved the flowers for the wind riders. The aircraft have been decorated with long trains of cut blooms and I can only imagine how amazing they're going to look once we're in the air.

Separate from the wind riders, a crowd of onlookers is gathering. I see several more Silfans, but also a few of those Winged-Ones, a big yeti-looking Dhugaren and some other aliens I haven't memorized the names of yet. None of them are flying, though. That realization is what makes the nerves finally set in. About this time, Prue would probably be telling me to really think about my choices, but she's not here. Instead, I search out Bazzel's recognizable shade of pink, spotting her quickly among the activity. I make my way towards her, smiling to myself as I see her pointing at people around her, obviously giving out orders.

"Hope! I'm glad you could make it. I already got a flyer ready for you. It's right next to mine, so I can show you the ropes," she shouts when she spots me approaching.

Her pink hair is pulled back in a deep indigo headband that compliments her rosy tones beautifully and her jumpsuit has been modified with a cinched belt and cropped sleeves. She's smiling brightly and standing with her hands on her hips like a superhero. She looks so in her element I want to take a picture, so I do.

Whipping my polaroid camera up from where it hangs around my neck, I snap a quick picture without stopping, grabbing the film as soon as it prints and shaking it.

"What in the station?" she says with wide eyes. I stifle a laugh at her euphemism.

"It's a camera. Y'all didn't have cameras on your planet?" I tease her.

"Of course we did, but they didn't print instantly," she exclaims. "Lemme see!"

I show her the image slowly coming into focus and she ahhs appropriately. When she reaches for it, though, I pull it back and tuck it into my breast pocket.

"Nope. It's mine. It's my art."

She rolls her eyes, but shrugs and leads me over to a pair of sturdy looking flyers.

"This one is mine, but the spare I found has the exact same controls so it'll be easy to teach you."

She shows me how to slide onto the platform under the sail on my belly and brace my feet on the lip at the end, then reach my arms out and hold the handlebars in front of me. Even being shorter than average, it's a tight squeeze and I have to bend my knees a bit and bring my elbows under me to fit, but it works. Probably not the safest thing I've ever done, but certainly not the most dangerous either.

Anyway, Bazzel doesn't look worried.

"I can totally do this," I tell her confidently.

She smiles wide and explains takeoff procedures to me quickly before pulling something from her breast pocket, "Almost forgot! I brought this for you. You're gonna want it up there."

She tosses me a bright scrap of fabric before taking off, waving down a passing Silfan male with a barked command. It's a vibrant marigold headband, the cloth soft and stretchy. I slip it over my neck, then pull it back over my forehead in a practiced move, pushing my wild bangs out of my face. I'm sure it looks silly, but Bazzel's right. I don't need my hair getting in my eyes when I'm fifty feet in the air.

It takes forever to get everyone in position and organized and not gossiping with each other, but *finally* we're ready to take off. The crowd has grown considerably and I'm desperately trying to ignore the voice that says I'm the only non-Silfan up here and I'm probably going to die, or worse, embarrass myself.

Then all of a sudden we're all running like a mad pack of exotic birds straight for the crowd of station citizens. I pump my arms frantically, making the sail flap like giant wings and the flyer picks up momentum along with the Silfans around me until I'm certain we'll run right into the people and cause a mass casualty incident that will go down in station history. Somewhere next to me, Bazzel whoops with delight.

When the first feeling of weightlessness starts in my belly, it's with relief and exhilaration both. I'm flying! It's a sensation I don't think I'll ever get used to, in the best way. As the meadows turn into a colorful grid below us and we rise higher into the air, I join the wind riders in whooping and shouting, sounds of elation rising up towards the artificial sun. Our trains create kaleidoscopes around us and I'm briefly devastated when I realize I can't get to my camera. The bulky thing is tucked into the side of my jumpsuit and unreachable in my current position.

Even the inability to capture the moment won't ruin it for me, though. I know I won't ever forget this and when I do finally get my hands on some art supplies this will be the first thing I paint. The fever dream of rainbow skies the Silfans have created and...him.

I don't see him at first, in the commotion, but as wind riders start to break off and spread out a flash of deep brown slips in and out of flower trains, like some elusive bird of prey.. When he's closer, I see that it's the same Winged-One who was volunteering in the meadows yesterday. His jumpsuit has been shredded into a pair of pants and a few scraps of fabric covering his chest, leaving his wings free to spread to their full span and it's massive. Easily six feet wide from claw to claw, he makes the wind riders look like tumbling toddlers, as clumsy as the *dersials* below us. He spins through the air like he was born there, twirling around me and zipping away with a mischievous smile. I laugh at his antics, my mood as weightless as I'm currently feeling.

Watching him fly, practically at his mercy as he flies circles around me—literally—I can't help but stare at his unique, strangely pleasing physique. His chest and shoulders are carved in lean, sinewy muscle. Beefy biceps lead to an elbow joint that tapers down into incredibly sharp looking claws. When he flies above me, the artificial sun shines through the translucent membrane of his wings, making them look like bronze

When the landing bell chimes, I want to ignore it. For the first time since we arrive, I feel like myself.

Landing is as exhilarating here as it was on Earth and it takes me a few moments to get my legs to stop shaking, so I smile at the Silfans who congratulate me, but I don't move to join their group quite yet. I'm not sure my knees won't buckle if I start walking. Also, as much as I hate to admit it, I might be a bit intimidated by them. Everyone else here seems to know each other already, and without Prue by my side introducing myself seems a lot harder.

"Wow, that was amazing! I have to try that someday," I hear a familiar voice say.

Coming towards me is a curvy, brunette, *human* woman. It's been days since I saw another human besides my sister, so it's kind of surprising at first. I'm even more shocked when I realize I know this woman.

"Hey! Pink sneakers! I know you. I've put your camera to good use." I wave the object in question from where it hangs around my neck.

She was the beautiful human being who traded me her polaroid camera for my old sneakers. I almost hadn't thrown the extra shoes in my duffel when Prue and I packed our go-bags, but she insisted on it. I was furious that she made me swap my watercolor set for the stupid things, but then it worked out for the best. The Originem probably would have confiscated the watercolors like they did my alcohol markers, but they let me keep the camera. All that's to say, I feel especially warm towards this particular human. So when I see she's holding hands with one of those big scary yeti aliens, I realize she may also be dickmatized—hypnotized by the aliens—and I'm going to have to save her.

"Maybe next week you can ride along with me. I've been trying to figure out how I can snap some photos up there, but flying takes both hands," I say, looking pointedly at their joined hands.

She frees herself and reaches in for a hug. I'm not a huge hugger, but I like this girl, so I pat her back a few times in what I hope is a friendly way.

"That sounds amazing. I'm Destiny by the way and," she takes a deep, audible breath, "this is my boyfriend, Khur."

Ah, fuck. It's worse than I thought. I smile and nod politely, but internally I'm freaking out. Am I the only woman here who hasn't lost their everloving mind? It can't be a coincidence that every human I know is pairing off with an alien. I mean, it's only two, but still...

"I'm Hope, and good for you. I haven't seen any interspecies couples yet, but humans are a bit freakier than most," I say, trying to stick to the truth. She looks really happy, so you know, good for her.

Destiny throws her head back and laughs, and it's so damn carefree and sweet I almost abandon my campaign to free her from whatever twisted shit our alien overlords are planning and join her instead.

"This is our boyfriend, too, Meshi," Khur tells me, gesturing to the Winged-One behind them I hadn't noticed before.

My eyebrows fly up of their own accord. I'm usually pretty good at hiding my reactions to proclamations like that—the art scene back home was fantastically eclectic like that—but I literally cannot help the look I shoot Destiny. I'm a little surprised this tiny, sweet thing could handle both—

"Oh, honey, no," Destiny exclaims. "That is a term of endearment between people who are courting. Meshi is just our *friend*."

Meshi is the same Winged-One that was flying with us earlier. This is like the third time I've seen him now and it's feeling a bit *purposeful*. Is this the alien the Originem have sent to seduce me and force-feed me whatever kool-aid they've got everyone else drinking? And more importantly, did they have access to my Kindle history at some point? Because they really did find my weakness. Something about the wings-for-arms things *does it* for me. Meshi's especially, because he has biceps and triceps—or whatever the Winged-One equivalent was—for days. His thick, corded wing muscles meet lithe, strong-looking shoulders, and through the shreds of fabric I'm pretty sure I also spot abs. Like, a lot of them. And all of it covered in dark brown velvety fur. I'm such a goner.

Then he opens his mouth.

"It is a true pleasure to meet you, beautiful Hope. When you flew, your radiance dimmed the light of the sun."

He holds out a clawed wing-tip and I gingerly shake it, dropping it quickly. I'm almost disappointed at how quickly he's proven my theory right. He's definitely here to seduce me. They may have gotten my physical type right, but nothing turns me off faster than an insincere compliment.

"Uhh, there's no sun here, but thanks."

"So, Hope, how did you get into flying? Gliding? What do the Silfans call it?" Destiny steps in and I shoot her a grateful look.

"They call it wind riding. Isn't that the coolest? I live on this division," I tell her, then shoot a look at Meshi. Probably shouldn't have dropped that tidbit, "and my neighbor invited me along. I hang-glided back at home so once they showed me the ropes it was easy to pick it up."

"You were a natural up there. The most radiant thing I've seen in an artificial sky," Meshi butts in, but I'm over it.

"You said that one already. I'm not interested, dude," I snap at him, honestly a little harsher than necessary. I almost feel bad when he curls his wings around his front as if to shield himself.

"Don't mind him. Meshi hasn't been around many humans yet. Maybe we can all get together for a picnic soon. I'm eager to meet more citizens. I haven't gotten to talk to many Silfans," Destiny gushes. "Really we could all benefit from mingling with other species."

"Sure," I reply, trying not to sound too sarcastic. Destiny is honestly the perfect candidate for a place like this. She's so open and unassuming, so naive in some ways. It's really sweet but it fills me with the need to protect her. She kind of reminds me of Prue, actually. They're both too trusting. We chat for a while but before they leave the meadows, I pull Destiny to the side and invite her over next week, using Prue's coffee as a bribe. Maybe if I can talk to her alone, apart from her new "boyfriend," I can convince her there's something fishy going on.

9

Meshi

"That was...less than ideal," Destiny says once we step onto the elevator. Khur looks at me sympathetically from behind her.

"That was a disaster," I reply morosely. "The worst first impression in Sanctuary history, possibly. Tell me truly, Destiny, have I ruined everything?"

"Nooo, Meshi! Where did you even hear that?" Destiny looks at me like I'm flying in circles, and maybe I am.

"Well, Josep told us that first impressions are very important to humans. I've been waiting for the perfect moment to introduce myself, and I completely crashed the landing."

It isn't til my claws tap the metallic floor of the elevator that I realize how much I'm letting my wings droop. It's an effort to straighten my spine and push my shoulders back, but I do it as the elevator dings our arrival back on division five. As we step out and turn left towards our subdivisions, I feel Destiny's small hand patting my shoulder affectionately.

"First impressions are important, but they aren't everything, Meshi. I'm sure Hope will love you when she sees the real you, not the schmoozeball who showed up at the Meadows earlier."

"I don't understand. That was the real me," I tell Destiny, "I meant every word I said."

"Wow, okay, you're...intense. That's cool, maybe just hold off on the showering-her-with-compliments thing until after you've gotten to know her a bit," Destiny says. "I mean, every girl is different, it just seems like Hope is a little more... wary. She invited me over for coffee next week. Why don't you come with me? It'll give you another chance to impress her."

"You're sure she wouldn't mind?"

"No way! We were just talking about how excited we are to meet new citizens and make friends. The more the merrier!" Destiny exclaims.

That sounds more like Destiny talking than Hope, but I would very much like another chance, and honestly, I don't really know her. I have no idea how she feels about meeting new people. So far, though, it doesn't seem positive.

"I'll go with you. I do not know what *coffee* is though."

"Oh, buddy. You're gonna love it."

With that settled, we part ways before we get into the heart of the market on our Division. Destiny and Khur slip through one of the side doors leading into their subdivision. I shoulder into the crowd, looking for the stall that's selling the fresh *pyongo* bread I'm smelling. I could go home and drown my feelings in carbs and maybe find one of those Dhugaren telenovelas to binge watch on my data pad.

I stop right in the middle of the market so quickly that a Dhugaren shoulder-checks me and mutters a rude name as they pass around me. I ignore them, though, because I realize I'm not ready to give up and binge on carbs and bad cinema. There's something I haven't tried yet, and I know this is what will woo my Hope. Turning on my claws, I jump into the air and fly back towards the elevators. Passing over the crowd is much quicker, and I need to get to division sixteen.

I don't come to the Winged-One's biome very often. I don't feel as connected to the dark, cool caves as my brothers and mother. It feels like a museum, a recreation of a lost part of our history, instead of the life-giving lungs of my people's culture. Is it because I was so young when we moved here? I don't think so. Other Winged-Ones my age do not seem to have the uncertainties that haunted me. Is it because I do not have a father to guide me? My mother has been filling the role my entire known life. I refuse to consider an explanation that makes her inadequate in any way.

The automatic doors hiss open and a cool breeze fills my wings. It smells like granite and moss. Our biome is an elaborate cave system, a labyrinth of stone filled with twists and turns, dead-ends and secret alcoves, with statues and wall-carvings on every corner. The younger kids like to play hide-and-seek in here and I can hear the excited screeching of someone being found as I make my way into the darkness.

Our sight isn't much better than anyone else, unfortunately, but our sonar abilities help us navigate the dim caverns. Every so often a *nifir*, the glowing crystal from our homeworld, light the main path, leading to the wide, tall chamber in the middle that is sometimes used for gatherings and celebrations. The route I'm looking for is one of the many inky black tunnels that shoot off this main one and it's been a while since I've visited. I almost miss it, but at the last second I click and see the carvings around the opening: rock and stone carved to look like clusters of crystals. As I swoop into the tunnel a group of children come running out. Three Winged-Ones hop, glide and run, unsteady on their wings still, their high pitch giggles filling the space.

"Scuse us!" the last one shouts at me as they barrel past. In the dim light it looks like he has something on his head and I click again, curious.

It's a Silfan child. Probably the same age as the other children, but much smaller by nature, the small child is riding on the shoulders of its friend, whooping and squealing as he clumsily tries to glide with the extra weight. I laugh out loud at the sight, and something settles, warm and cozy, in my heart. This is the world the Originem imagined. This is the world we're all trying to build. It feels like a sign, and I am not one to ignore such things. With renewed purpose, I make my way deeper into the tunnel.

10

Hope

I sort of...forget to tell Prue about inviting Destiny for coffee. There was so much excitement with the flying and to be fair, she hasn't been home much. So this morning when I walk in the kitchen and she's standing at the chemical-stained counter cleaning a pretty ceramic tray and mugs with a rag—where did she even find any of that shit?—I realize, I may have fucked up.

"So, Pruuue," I say sweetly, walking into the kitchen to stand beside her. "You know how you were saying I need to get out there and make friends?"

"No. I don't remember saying that." She looks at me suspiciously. "What did you do?"

"That's not fair! Who says I did anything? Besides invite another friend over for coffee today. She's human," I rush to add, like it would make any difference.

"Hope are you fucking— You know what. It's fine. It's already done now. At least I have four mugs." She turns away from me and picks up another mug, its blue-glazed surface already shining perfectly, and twists the rag viciously around its rim. “Go straighten up the living room.”

"Okayyy.” *Mom.* I add silently.

In the living room, everything is in order. I put the data pad thing that I haven't even opened on Prue's bed and boom. The exact same gray-washed common room we found when we arrived. If someone accidentally walked in our apartment they'd think it’s vacant. It makes me want to cry. I am no closer to finding art supplies after almost two weeks living on Sanctuary Station and that is deeply depressing. I've been spending a lot of time at the Meadows, though, and Bazzel has been teaching me the intricacies of gardening—the Silfan way. Not getting to fly today kind of sucks, but this meeting is important. I need to get a handle on this alien who's swept in and took Prue from me so efficiently. Maybe with Destiny separated from her own alien, she’ll see the game for what it is. Some big Originem chess board that we’re only pawns on.

While I ponder the conspiracies of deep space, fluffing the couch cushions just to keep my hands busy, a chime sounds at the door, letting us know someone is standing there. Automatic doorbells, really the Originem have thought of everything.

Prue runs in from the kitchen before I've made two steps in the direction of the door, beating me there and waving her wrist over the panel in a haste. The door slides open and reveals a freakishly tall, green, Amazon warrior lady. Well, let's hope she means well towards my sister because this woman could probably kill me with a solid slap to the face.

She has two strips of beige fabric tied around her breasts and waist, fashioned into a tube top and mini skirt, and wears nothing else. From her surprisingly human-shaped, bright green feet, to the well-defined muscles of her abdomen, Prue's girlfriend looks like she stepped out of a jungle and accidentally landed on a space station. Even her hair, which looks like long, thick vines, seems to sway to an unseen breeze.

"Asper! You made it! I'm so, so happy you're here," Prue gushes.

Coming on a little strong, aren't we sis? I think, but outwardly I smile towards the alien being ushered into our living room.

"This is my sister, Hope. Hope, this is Asper." She positions us in front of each other in that awkward way people do and I barely resist putting my hand out to shake. Even I know that is a human thing.

"Pleasure to meet you," I say stiffly instead.

"The pleasure is shared, Hope. Your sister has told me so much about you. I would love for you to come visit the Jungle, soon. I can teach you Ferziti basket braiding. It's not painting, but it is good to make things with your hands all the same," Asper says in a voice much softer than I expect.

My hindbrain is screaming, *trick.* It's telling me not to trust it, but Asper seems so sincere. She's looking down at me with these big hopeful eyes and I get the impression she's a gentle giant. She's wringing her hands for fucks sake. This is not a conspiratorial mastermind. I grimace.

"That sounds really lovely. I didn't know there's a jungle on the station. Why don't we sit down and you can tell me about it." I sound so stiff, so weird. I know I do. I'm not used to people looking to me for approval like this. I get the impression that she really cares what I think. I can't relate, honestly, but it's so cute how Prue takes one of her huge hands and holds it in her smaller ones. I can see their happiness and it makes me...uncomfortable. I push the feeling away before I have to process it.

Luckily, I'm saved by the doorbell.

"Hiii! Thanks for having me," Destiny is all smiles as she sweeps in the door like the leader of a monster conga line, being followed by two towering Dhugarens and—seriously?! —that Meshi guy, again.

"Hey, Destiny, who's all this?" I ask, with maybe a bit more bite than I intended. I just got done telling Prue that it was only one other human, and now she's walking in here with half the crew of the Enterprise. I can't control the slight frustrated tilt of my head, though I'm sure others would say I 'have an attitude.'

Destiny, of course, being this little ball of sunshine that is starting to look a *little* less shiny, doesn't notice it. She beams at everyone and starts introductions.

"Well, this is Khur, my... partner. And Meshi, our friend, I believe you've met before, Hope," she says, giving me a *look*. Traitor. "And this is my best friend, Furga. She loves meeting new citizens, too. How do your people greet each other, do you shake hands?"

Destiny extends a hand and looks at Asper expectantly, who in turn looks wildly uncomfortably between Destiny's face, her hand and Prudence. Prudence shoots *me* a look that could burn my eyebrows off and that's when I realize that this is going to be the most disastrous coffee date in the history of the galaxy.

A long, uncomfortable moment passes before a patient voice speaks up from our still-open door. "I believe only humans shake hands, Destiny." Meshi glides through the living room, where we've all bunched up awkwardly, and moves towards the couches, closing the gap between the new arrivals and Prue and Asper. When he is in front of them, he makes a strange gesture like he is swiping his nonexistent hair behind his ear, then folds his hand into a fist on his heart before sitting on one of the couches across from them. Thank goodness we configured it for a "roomier" setup instead of the more minimal settings. And also thank goodness for Prue and her tech-savvy ways. I am so hopeless when it comes to that kind of thing.

"Well met, friends, my name is Meshi," he says to the two women on the couch in a sweet, serene voice. It is different from what I expect of him, the simpering fool from last week completely gone.

The difference in Asper is immediate. She must be comforted by that little bit of familiarity because she repeats the gesture back to him and says, "Well met. I am Asper. This is my partner, Prue."

My sister blushes furiously and I have no control over the smile that touches my own lips. I love seeing her happy. Meshi catches my eye with a secretive smile as Destiny '*awws*' at my side and it all feels *too* sweet. Too perfect. Like an after-school special, all of us kumbaya-ing like that. It's not *real*. It can't be. And even though I see the way that Asper looks at Prudence and I know that she isn't pretending to be absolutely smitten, even though I see how Khur's eyes get all big and shiny when he looks at Destiny too long, I can't help but think it's all too good to be true.

"So, how about that coffee?" I ask everyone, perhaps a touch too loudly.

"We can get that!" Prue says, jumping up and pulling Asper with her. It's almost comical to see my sister, only a few inches taller than me, trying to pull the much taller woman up, but Asper rises with a smile meant for only her and that strange twinge in my chest makes itself known again. I think I might have a heart condition.

"Wow, I've never seen one of those before!" The Dhugaren woman, Furga, exclaims once they've disappeared into the kitchen.

"The Ferziti people are very reclusive. I've helped with maintenance on the humidity controls on their division before," Meshi says, using that calm, confident voice again. "This isn't your first rotation on the space station, Furga. Have some tact."

"I'm just excited, that's all!" she responds, "Destiny wants to meet all the different species here. I'm trying to help."

"We are all citizens of the same home," he replies, unruffled.

There's something about his collected confidence that makes me feel a little better, like I can take a full breath and relax, a tiny bit. He seems so *chill*, like nothing could phase him. I envy it. My anxiety is constantly beating against my skin, screaming to get out, run away, something bad is going to happen any minute now. But Meshi has his claws folded neatly in his lap and he offers me a calming smile when our eyes meet. I feel the corners of my mouth lift in return, miniscully. His smile brightens to a megawatt that leaves me temporarily stunned, and luckily I'm saved by my sister and Asper walking back out with a tray of mugs and a metal carafe.

"There aren't enough mugs for everyone, so we'll have to share. Destiny and Khur do you mind?" My sister asks as she starts filling mugs with a dark, steaming liquid.

"Of course not," Destiny replies, all smiles.

"Hope and I will share," says the confident voice on the couch and I suppress a shiver at the sound of my name. I will *not* lose my self-control because some alien with a deep, self-assured voice says my name. I will also *not* consider the fact that our lips will both touch the rim of the mug if we share. I should speak up, say I'll share with Furga, but she looks pretty furry. I don't love the idea of hair in my coffee.

"Sure," I say when I realize everyone is looking at me.

"Be careful," Asper says as she passes Meshi the mug. "It's hot."

His claws are surprisingly dexterous as he grips the mug and brings the steaming cup to his face, inhaling deeply.

"I've never had anything like coffee."

"Dhugarens are fond of a hot drink," Furga says, taking her cup and blowing on it loudly.

I sit awkwardly next to Meshi, since we're sharing a drink and I *really* want some caffeine. His jumpsuit has been deconstructed, sleeves cut away and armholes lengthened to fit his wings. They look soft, like velvet, and I want to run my palm across their membranes. I bite the inside of my cheek. *Bad Hope.*

Furga settles next to Asper and Prue on the couch across from us and Khur perches on the armrest, pulling Destiny onto his massive thigh. We all sit and enjoy our steaming drinks for a few minutes, with us human women making only slightly obscene sounds when the hot, nutty liquid touches our tongues. There's really nothing like a warm drink full of caffeine to energize the soul.

"Destiny, let me show you how to get hot water out of your nutritional printer and I can send you home with some of the ground *subus* to make for yourself," Prue says, hopping up from the couch. She smiles down at Asper, who seems to be in a lively discussion with Furga about ceramics, then leads Destiny and Khur into the kitchen.

I turn towards Meshi, who I've been awkwardly avoiding looking towards this whole time. He's acting like a totally different person then the weird guy from the meadows last week, but when he looks at me with those intense, darker-than-coffee eyes I still feel too seen, too well observed, like he is gazing right inside my mind. I start talking in an attempt to break the spell he's casting on me.

"Why do they call you guys 'Winged-Ones'? Don't your people have a name for, well.. Your people?" I ask him, offering the mug back to him with two hands.

"Yes. It is...complicated. Winged-One is a translation of my language. It's like..." he pauses, taking a drink and contemplating his words, "your world had multiple languages, right?"

"Yeah? I mean, don't they all?"

"No, but mine does and that's the point here. Try to say something in another language. Other than your own," he tells me, handing the mug back again.

For some unholy reason the only thing I can think of is a french lyric from an old musical my mom loved to watch when all our menstrual cycles synced up, and I blurt out, "*Voulez-vous coucher avec moi, ce soir.*"

The way the corner of his lip quirks up and he looks over at me from the side of his eye without completely turning his head, but tilts that adorable oversized ear closer to me as if he doesn't want to miss a single word I say has my stomach doing backflips around my kidneys. It also has me re-evaluating the last minute of conversation and realizing that he clearly understood everything I said to him. More, in fact, than I did, because I do not speak French. I have no clue what I said.

Oh god! I think that musical was about a brothel! What did I say?! Am I sitting here gaping like a fish because his fangs stick out of his bottom lip when he smiles like that and I can't stop staring at it?

"Khur told me that humans have many euphemisms for copulation. Winged-Ones are the same. Taking an afternoon flight, flapping the northern wing, uncoiling the rope, playing a little bind and seek, tying the midnight knots—"

"Oh my god, enough!" I hiss, my face a burning flame. "Why do you have so many bondage euphemisms?"

Meshi brings a clawed wing-tip up between our faces, which I notice have gotten very close, and runs a sharp digit down my jaw. "With things like these, we have to get... creative."

My brain completely short circuits. I make the most embarrassing sound in my life—something like *hnnghh*—as I feel my panties instantly flood with wetness. For a moment I think my knees are going to buckle, before the cocky, arrogant, smarmy, stupid alien sits back, pulling his claw away and smirking at the obvious effect he has on me. My EMP'ed brain is scrambling for some smart-ass remark to even our playing fields again, when I hear Prue scream from the kitchen.

It's an excited, happy scream, but Asper obviously doesn't know that because she bolts up from the couch, spilling *subus* on the chrome floors in her haste. Oblivious to the mess, she turns towards the kitchen, but Prue, Destiny and Khur are already coming back into the living room. Prue and Destiny are both smiling from ear to ear and holding hands with white-knuckled excitement.

"We have the most amazing news, everyone!" Destiny announces to the room, reaching behind her to grab Khur's big paw.

Prue beckons Asper closer and the nervous-looking green woman quietly makes her way over to my sister, standing behind her with an arm possessively around her chest. To me, it looks like Asper is using Prue as a shield, and I privately re-assess their dynamics. Prue has always been the one who handles the paperwork, the back office drudgery, the forms and permits, so seeing her front and center is a little weird. It feels wrong and I can't help but think that Prue needs someone to protect her, not the other way around.

Before I can speak up, though, Prue and Destiny exchange a look—their hands are still clasped like they're great friends—and then blurt three words that shake the foundation of my entire world.

"We're both pregnant!"

The room erupts into activity, Furga immediately jumps up and wraps Prue and Destiny in a huge, fuzzy hug, while Asper and Khur awkwardly pat each other's backs and offer each other congratulations. Next to me, Meshi grabs the ceramic mug, still half-full of the precious caffeinated liquid, and throws it on the ground with a high-pitched clicking sound. It shatters, pieces of ceramic going everywhere and coffee splashing the legs of my jumpsuit. The entire room makes an audible gasp. As if underwater, I turn my head slowly towards him and squint. I get the feeling any moment now everyone is going to shout 'gotcha!' or maybe I'll wake up.

Meshi's face, lit up with a joyous smile, falls slightly when he realizes the room has gone silent. "I'm so sorry about that. It's a Winged-One tradition. If you're holding a drink when someone announces they're pregnant, you throw it on the ground to fertilize their blessing." He looks down at the mess he made, scratching the back of his hairless head with a sharp claw. "I guess that doesn't make a lot of sense here."

"Meshi, it's brilliant, I love it." Destiny says, then she rears back and Babe Ruth pitches the mug she's holding into the ground with as much strength as she can muster. The ceramic and *subus* volcano out in all directions, covering both of the happy couples as well as a good portion of our couch.

"NO!" Prue shouts, but it's too late. The mess is made.

My sisters anguished shout seems to trigger something in Asper though, because in a blink the tall female transforms, her viney hair sticking out in all directions like a bush and her arms stick-straight at her sides. Her skin changes before our eyes, turning into the mottled brown of tree bark. It takes a few blinks to understand what just happened.

"Did she just turn into a tree?" I shout at my sister. This is getting weirder and weirder.

"Great Ulvand, I think she did!" Furga shouts back, practically hopping up and down with excitement. "That's the coolest thing I've ever seen!"

Next to Prue, Destiny is wringing her hands, desperately trying to apologize, while behind her, Khur is starting to look a bit like a polar bear trapped in a cage, dark eyes darting back and forth like he's searching for an escape.

"It's okay, she really needs a calm and quiet environment so she can un-camouflage herself," Prue murmurs.

She has her hands up as if to ward everyone away from them. Behind her, tree-Asper's leaves are quivering dramatically. Her face is barely discernible in the patterns of the bark, her eyes squeezed shut.

Khur has started panting rather noisily and Destiny shifts her attention to calming him down, in a loud, clear voice. Prue looks like she is going to have an aneurysm any moment now, a vein on the left side of her temple visibly throbbing. Furga is still exclaiming her excitement over meeting a tree-person, and next to me, Meshi is the only one with the presence of mind to be quiet for a minute. He's standing close enough for our arms to brush. I cast him a scathing glare. He has the gall to look remorseful, his soft-looking ears drooping with regret. He started this, the big idiot, and now I'm going to have to clean it up. Prue may not like it, but she needs someone like me around, and I'm about to prove that to her. She needs someone to look out for her and protect her, and obviously Asper is not capable of doing that.

"Shut the fuck up!" I shout, making my voice project as much as I can.

It does the job of shocking everyone into shutting the fuck up, but for some reason Destiny and Prue both immediately stab me with their angry glares. Beside them, Khur has started to wheeze and mutter, covering his face with his huge, meaty palms, and tree-Asper is shaking like she's been caught in an invisible storm. So dramatic.

"You're not helping, Hope," Prue hisses at me, awkwardly rubbing Asper's stiff arms.

"Well, I'm trying, aren't I? I'm not the one who turned into a tree! Why would you announce it like that?" I hiss back, jabbing my finger in her direction.

"I didn't—I meant to—" Prue starts and stops a few times, looking between me and

tree-Asper like she can't stand to look away from her for a second. "I tried to tell you, like twenty times over the last week. I just couldn't figure out what to say."

"You've been hiding this the whole fucking week? Are you serious Prue? Did you even know she was a tree, or is this new to you, as well?"

Prue steps towards me, her face transformed into something livid.

"Don't say another word about Asper. She's amazing and you're just *jealous*," she sneers at me, emphasizing her point with a vicious finger in my chest. "You're jealous because she's taking up my time and my priorities instead of you."

Her words ring too close to the truth for comfort. Am I jealous of my sister's girlfriend? She's never really had a serious relationship before, but that's because she never wanted one. Why has that changed now?

"It's like I don't even know you anymore."

"Hope..." The way she says my name makes me freeze. "I'm starting to think...maybe you don't. Maybe you haven't really known me for a while."

She sighs long and loud, her brow bunching with worry when she glances back at tree-Asper once more.

"Listen, I think you should go."

On the other side of the room, Destiny is talking to Khur in a sweet, calm voice. Furga has finally chilled out enough to be useful and is carrying two glasses—the station-issued ones, sadly—of water to him and tree-Asper. Even Meshi is cleaning up the gigantic mess he and Destiny made with a towel he found in the bathroom.

"I was trying to help," I plead, my voice small. I hate how pathetic I sound.

"I know, but, I think you've done enough. Just, please leave before things get worse." She's already turning away from me, towards tree-Asper. "I need to focus on her right now, okay?"

"I don't have anywhere else to go." I whisper. How is this even my fault? I didn't throw the stupid mugs on the floor.

"Hope!" Prue snaps. "Not...UGH... not forever, just go to the meadows for an hour or something. We'll go to Asper's for the night. You and I...we'll talk later, okay? I just can't deal with you right now."

That last hit lands right where she aimed, right in my chest. It's always been Hope and Prue, til the end, but now she's kicking me to the curb for someone she met a week ago. I can feel everyone's eyes on me as I turn towards the door. A clawed hand grabs my elbow before I can reach the door. Meshi's eyes are filled with pity and it twists the knife in my chest even further. I wrench my arm away.

"Hope, wait. I'm here if you want to talk to anyone," he implores.

"I don't even know you, creep! Leave me alone!" My voice rises an octave at the end and I clap a hand over my mouth, running out the door before anyone else can stop me.

11

Meshi

I want to follow Hope out of the apartment. I want to find her and wrap my wings around her and figure out exactly why she is so upset about her sister's announcement. Does she not like children? That would be unfortunate, because I have always wanted a big family. Or perhaps she does not like Asper. I admit, sometimes Furga is not my favorite person, but Shemo has chosen her as his life partner and I want my brother to be happy more than anything else.

I don't know the answers to these questions, but I am starting to understand my Hope a bit more. I think her sister should not have told her such big news in front of an audience. I could tell that she did not appreciate me stopping her. She wouldn't want to look vulnerable in front of all these other people. I should not have offered my assistance so blatantly either, but I'm still learning how to handle my tiny human.

So as much as I want to follow her out into the greater Division and ask her how she's feeling, I refrain.

Hope is like the geode I'm carving. She's hard and rough on the inside, but I know if I can get past those outermost layers, there is so much beauty and depth beneath. Like carving geodes, though, I must be patient, careful. I can't force it, can't hammer away and expect the results I desire. That's why Winged-Ones are so good at carving geodes. Our claws are made for precision, for finding the intricacies hidden within. So even though I want to chase after her and insist she talk to me, I don't.

Instead, I stay and finish cleaning up the mess I made. I feel terrible for breaking Prue's new drinkware, but at the same time I feel oddly proud of myself. I threw down the cup without even thinking, so happy for my new friends. It pleases me to know that I am Winged-One enough to offer a traditional congratulations without even thinking about it. It makes me want to share even more.

"Prue, if I may," I start. "I wanted to apologize again for breaking your mugs. I would like to make it up to you."

"Hey, Meshi, right?" Hope's sister smiles at me, but her forehead is almost as ridged as mine is, so I know she's still upset. "It's okay. Furga was telling me she knows a Dhugaren ceramicist who makes dinnerware."

"Yes, Rugarra is brilliant with her hands," I reply. "I cannot make a new cup, but I would like to make you something for your new little one. A traditional Winged-One gift if you do not mind."

"Why would I mind? That sounds amazing," Prue turns to Asper with watery eyes.

The Ferziti is still frozen in camouflage, the stiff vines of their hair reminiscent of branches of a tree.

"She's actually really great, you know," Prue whispers so quietly I almost don't hear her. "She just has anxiety. I thought Hope, of all people, would understand that."

Prue gazes up at Asper with a look so adoring, so vulnerable, I have to look away. Next to us, Furga has taken a towel and is sopping up the muddy liquid extending around me like debris from an explosion. The bottom of my pants are soaked and little droplets of dark grey speckle up my legs.

"She seems lovely. I can't wait to get to know you both better," I console her, barely refraining from telling her we'll all be family one day soon. "You two are going to make wonderful parents."

By the door, Destiny is rubbing Khur's massive forearm—the closest thing the tiny human can probably reach. He's calmed down from his panic attack, but my Dhugaren friend still looks upset and I remember belatedly that Khur has PTSD from his previous life on the Dhugarens' war-ridden, autocratic home planet. He was probably triggered by the loud noise of my breaking mug.

I really made a mess of things.

12

Hope

By the time I reach the meadows, I'm gasping for breath. When I ran out of our apartment, my adrenaline was up and I sprinted all the way here. I have no clue where anything else is on this stupid space station, so it was the obvious destination. The meadows are exactly where I need to be, though, because as soon as I walk in my lungs get a taste of that fresh, floral air and I can finally breathe again. There's something so peaceful about being in this eternally Spring biome. One really could believe that when they step through the doors, they're stepping outside. I bet they even have some kind of Vitamin D light, because the warm pseudo-sunlight always makes me happy.

Slowly walking further into the biome with my hands on my hips, I can feel my blood pressure dropping as my breaths even out. With each lung-burning breath my anger fades a little more. What replaces it is an ugly, stinging feeling. I recognize how ridiculous it is to feel betrayed that my sister is pregnant, but we *just* got here. Like, how do they even know this early? Not to mention the mechanics...I don't want to think too hard about that, though.

I scuff my feet at the ground, dropping my arms and looking around now that I've burned some of my anger away. The harvested fields are closer to the entrance this week. The flyers are long gone and the crowds dispersed already, but their flower trains were all left behind in soft-looking piles among the shortly cut fields. I eye the closest flower mound, considering the possibility of a little nap.

"Hey, Hope! I thought you weren't coming out today."

A familiar pink figure walks towards me, a burlap sack slung over her shoulder. Bazzel's hair is pushed back by an emerald green hairband today and it accentuates her rosy tones nicely.

"Hey! I wasn't planning on it, but here I am," I tell her. "You're not hand-harvesting *dersials* again are you?"

"What? Oh this?" She gestured to the bag across her back. "No, I'm gathering petals. They make gorgeous sun catchers."

Any thoughts of napping disappear completely.

"Wait, are you telling me that you're an artist?" I ask her, buzzing with excitement.

"This word doesn't translate. What is *artist*?" She sounds the word out strangely, like she's never heard it before.

"What do you mean? Silfans don't have art? Painters or sculpturists or anything?"

Bazzel raises her bright pink eyebrows at me and I get the impression the *are-you-stupid?* look is universal.

"We have art. And we have plenty of creators. We don't have a word for someone who is art. Everyone is art. Everyone can make art. If creating art is your calling and you don't have a specialty or preferred medium, you might be called a creator, but most Silfans consider themselves creators from time to time. You should read my dad's love poems."

She explains all this while leading me towards one of the piles of petals. They remind me of the Autumns of my childhood. We used to rake dead leaves into big piles in the fall and jump in them. While I consider her words, she starts to pick out big petals of fuschia and deep indigo.

"That's an interesting concept," I concede, "but how do you create now? With no paint or canvas or even some sketching paper? It's tyrannical!"

She looks at me pointedly before looking back down at the flowers piled before us.

"We make it work. We get creative." Bazzel's tone is sharp and I can see the resemblance to Harrow for the first time. "We remind each other how thankful we are for the opportunity to be here. We owe the Originem our lives. Our home planet, Esprit, is completely inaccessible to us. So a few rules may be annoying, but we will follow them gladly."

My first instinct is to snap at Bazzel. *I don't owe them anything.* That's not really true, though. If they hadn't found us, Prue and I would have died on the roof of that highrise apartment, with water lapping at our feet. They never forced us to do anything. Everything was presented as a choice, and when Prudence chose this place, I followed her.

It's extremely frustrating to realize I may have been a *teensy* bit unreasonable in my demand for art supplies. The back of my mind nudges me; there may be something else I was a *teensy* bit unreasonable about, too. I'm not ready to think about that yet, and I am certainly not ready to talk about my sister's *big news* with anyone yet. So instead I bend down and pick up a particularly bright fuschia petal as big as my palm and hold out my offering tentatively.

"Will you tell me more about your suncatchers?"

Bazzel describes how she presses the petals dry and then cuts tiny geometric patterns in them before setting each one in a thin disc of resin-like material and chaining them together. When the sun—well, the artificial lights of our space station—shines through, they cast colorful, kaleidoscopic patterns on the ground. I help her find the most intact flower petals that will work best with her project as she describes her methods and a peace comes over me that I haven't felt in over a year. The peace of being surrounded by color, helping with an art project, and hearing a friend talk passionately about their work.

Have I been too presumptive? Did I jump to conclusions being so suspicious of the Originem? The jury is still out, but I can admit that art and artists are more prevalent than I'd originally believed. Our "benevolent alien overlords" could have made it easier on us, given the humans better resources to acclimate to life on the space station a little more seamlessly. With Prue's news, I am still on the fence about the Originems motives, but no matter how I try to wrap my mind around it, I can't place soft-spoken Asper in any kind of sinister plot.

I eyeball Bazzel speculatively as we walk to another field, this one piled with shorn flowers of cerulean and burnt orange. She is a good foot and a half shorter than me, but she carries herself with confidence and ease. Here in the Meadows, she is obviously in her element, and I long for a bygone time when I was walking through Hyde Park like that. Like I was completely comfortable in my body and my surroundings.

I've been thrown into so many scary new situations in the last year—we all have—and I think it's finally catching up with me. Maybe, just maybe, I've been lashing out at the wrong people since we arrived here on Sanctuary. The thought sits heavy in my gut.

We gather flowers for a while longer in thoughtful silence. I'm not one who usually does well with silence, but every time I open my mouth to speak, I close it again. I find myself not wanting to offend my new friend, which is uncharted territory for me, but I can't seem to summon the blind faith that she has. I can't help that I'm a pessimist at heart.

By the time we make our way back to the fields closest to the door, our fingers are stained and our faces shine with a fine layer of sweat. I feel better than I have in months, and I rub the pads of my purple-tinged fingertips together thoughtfully.

"Hey, do you mind if I take a few petals? A handful. I just had an idea," I ask Bazzel.

"Sure," she replies, reaching into her burlap sack. "I had a feeling you might get inspired today, if you let yourself be open to it."

Her smile is genuine as she holds out some of the prettiest petals we found today, and though the urge to get offended rises in me, I push it down as well as I can. I did get inspired today, even if it came from a somewhat uncomfortable place. Any good artist knows that's where the best inspiration comes from, but damn if it wasn't especially excruciating this time.

"Thank you, Bazzel." I turn to leave, holding the petals delicately in my stained hands. Something stops me, though, some toxic urge that just can't let things go, and I turn back one more time. "Wait! Can I ask you one thing, I just need someone else's opinion."

"Of course. What is it, Hope?" She tilts her head and her pink hair falls in a silky straight waterfall across her shoulder as she waits for me to speak.

"Do you know of any couples from different species? Is that a common thing here?" My voice betrays me, the way it wavers. Am I...scared for my sister? For my soon-to-be niece or nephew? I won't let the Originem experiment on her, no matter how benevolent they say they are.

"Oh, my friend," Bazzel's eyes go soft and sympathetic as she draws closer, putting a hand on my elbow—the closest thing she can reach to patting my back I assume, "here on Sanctuary, everyone just wants you to be happy. I don't know of any inter-species couples myself, but I promise you, no one would judge you for loving someone. We've all been through enough already to waste time with that."

Oh, god. She thinks I'm asking for *myself*?! That's crazy! And why do Meshi's earlier words pop in my mind right at this moment—*With things like these, we have to get... creative*—and the click of those wickedly sharp looking claws, the way he would have to be so gentle with me.

Holy Shit, Hope! Get it together. I am asking for my sister, for her safety. I am going to have to protect her and Asper, because Asper is part of this family now. It is certainly going to take some getting used to, but if I have to choose between Prue and Asper, or no one, the choice is obvious. Like Bazzel said, we've all been through enough already to waste any more time judging other people.

I nod, not bothering to explain, then pull my friend in for a quick hug. She makes a surprised sound—I'm kind of surprised myself, I'm not a natural hugger—before embracing me in return. Her cheek is pressed against my belly and her arms are wrapped around my butt, but it doesn't feel lewd or weird, it feels soothing, like a balm against my battered spirit.

"Thank you, Bazzel," I tell her sincerely. "I'm really glad we met. You're a good friend."

"You're not so bad, yourself, Hope," she responds. "It's going to take some time to acclimate to a world where everything really is what it seems to be."

When I leave the Meadows, I feel both better and worse than when I first arrived. It's probably a sign of personal growth or whatever, but right now it's an achy, unwanted feeling that I'm still digesting. I'm definitely not ready to go back to the apartment, empty or not.

I didn't plan to ever go back to the scene of my crime, but it's getting late and the lights have been dimmed for the "sleep-cycle." Insert eye roll. I haven't explored this division—aka the floor we live on, insert *another* eye roll, please—very much at all and I don't know where much is, but I remember where my "artivism" is, and it seems like the perfect place to think, and maybe have a good cry while I'm there.

I'm kind of surprised that the Originem have left it up. For some reason, I expected it to be gone, not a speck left behind on a perfectly blank wall, like any other good big brother overlord would do, but there she is, in all her glory. What truly captures my attention, though, and makes the tears that had been threatening for a while now finally spill over, is what surrounds the woman in my mural. Handprints, paw prints, claw prints, I even think I see a few hoofprints on the wall nearest the floor, and one long tentacle print arches above her head, each sucker standing out in stark relief, like a polka-dotted rainbow. The prints are all made from different mediums, some bright, opaque colors that look like acrylic paint, others are flat shades of black and grey, mottled like a damp ink pad might do.

They surround my artwork from all sides, but none overlap her, none cover the brushes and pens I'd painted. It feels like they are offering solidarity, and somehow it feels like maybe they are offering safety to this imaginary woman, and the space to express her emotions. They have created a cocoon of love around her, and simultaneously answered the plea I painted.

When my tears blur my vision too much to keep looking, I press my back to the mural and slide down the wall, pulling my knees to my chest. I guess this is gonna be my mental breakdown hallway now.

13

Meshi

The party ended hours ago, but I haven't gone home yet. I found excuses to stay on this division, first checking on the nutritional printers I fixed last week, then popping in to check on Jerrol's ankle. Both were doing fine and I could only "catch up" with Jerrol and Harrow for so long before the silence between conversations became awkward.

I don't know why I linger here. Hope isn't going to seek me out and if I were to run into her in the corridors she would not welcome my company. It's clear to me she does not yet feel the chemistry between us, but I cannot fathom how to change that. Her carving won't be complete for weeks—it's a complex and meticulous process—but I can't wait that long to speak to her, to be in her presence.

Division 12's lights have dimmed to indicate the sleep cycle as I've wandered their endless corridors. Each division is the size of a city, though much of the space on each division is residential by necessity. One could walk the public corridors all night and not cover an entire division. Somehow, I find myself heading towards the place I first saw Hope, painting her mural with passion and fury.

As I approach, my sensitive hearing picks up a sniffling sound. I tuck into the shadows and peek around the corner.

There, curled up right underneath her masterpiece, is the woman who's turned my mind inside out. All thoughts of my own distress flee, though, when I see that she is crying. Her head jerks up as soon as I step out of the shadow and she wipes furiously at her wet face with the long sleeves of her jumpsuit. Keeping my movements slow and steady, like I'm approaching a wild animal, I lower myself onto the ground next to her, resting my back against the wall and bringing my wings around to rest on my crossed knees. Tilting my head back, I lean against the wall and close my eyes. Then, I wait.

She doesn't immediately jump up and run away or lash out at me, so I'll take it as a win. The cool metal of the floor and wall against my bare arms is refreshing. The faintly chemical smell of Hope's mural, and the rest of the stations' artful contributions tickles my nose. I catalog all these sensations and let them pass, like a gentle breeze. Still, Hope sits next to me. She settles back against the wall and mirrors my pose, sighing loudly.

"Do you know who did this?" she asks after a few minutes, gesturing to the wall behind us.

"I assume you mean the prints?" I question her, turning my head to the side to look at her.

"Yeah. The handprints and stuff." She looks tired. Dark circles line the bottom of her deep brown eyes and though she isn't crying anymore, her face is red and tender-looking. My heart aches for her.

"I believe Division 12's primary class took a field trip here a few days ago," I tell her, recounting the gossip Jerrol had imparted upon me while I was visiting earlier. "Their instructor wanted them to see an example of art in action. From what I understand, the children were very moved by your plight and wanted to help. What you see up there are examples of the many different materials citizens have repurposed or made to suit their needs."

"What?" she chokes out, looking at me like she might cry again.

"They wanted you to know about what they use to paint, so you would be able to use them, too," I rush to explain. "I know you probably can't tell just by looking at them, but I can help you figure out what they all are, if you'd like."

She sniffles, nodding her head in a human gesture that means she agrees.

"Thank you, Meshi," she mutters, her voice thick with emotion. "I'm... sorry. I've been really mean to you and here you are offering to help me. That's really nice."

I forgive you! I would do anything for you! I want to tell her, but I manage to hold it in.

"I can't imagine how hard this transition must be for you," I explain instead. "I was just a kit when my family moved here, and I still struggle sometimes."

"Really? You seem so comfortable here."

"Don't get me wrong, Sanctuary Station is my home. I just—" I search for the right words, surprised I'm even talking about this right now, "I guess I just struggle to find the balance between Winged-One and Sanctuary citizen."

She turns towards me, giving me her full attention. "I totally get that."

"I've been finding ways to connect to my heritage more lately, actually," I murmur, letting my mouth lift in a smile. "I've had an idea for a project I'd love your help with."

"My help? What could I possibly help with?"

"Well, word around the station is you're a pretty talented artist in need of a project," I said, "and I have a project in desperate need of an artistic touch."

Hope giggles and it transforms her entire being. Her cheeks round and her eyes squint adorably. She looks so much lighter than she did moments ago.

"It seems like I got what I wanted, after all," she tells me, still smiling softly. "Maybe I'm a tad bit impulsive. It's something I'm working on... Anyways, tell me about this project."

"Well, we call them *minklas*. We make them for Winged-One children, to hang above their cribs. They're usually made of carved crystals and other bobbles that fracture the light and create patterns on the walls for the kits to look at." I pause, letting Hope process that, because she's no idiot and she will see where this is going.

"That sounds beautiful, Meshi."

Her voice is a whisper, but I suppress a shiver when she says my name nonetheless.

"I—I would really like to help you make a *minkla*," she murmurs. "Maybe we could make two?"

Her face, full of hesitant hope, guts me. Here is a woman who has been let down too many times. I'm not going to let it happen again.

"I think that's a great idea."

As if now that's decided, she can relax, Hope leans back against the wall, but she scoots closer to me and leans her arm against my wing, tilting her head as if to lay it on my shoulder.

"Wait," I say, then quickly wrap my wing around her before she thinks I'm rebuking her. She lays her head against my chest and I cover her with my warm embrace. I am honestly shocked at the turn of events. I have no clue what I've done to finally entice my woman into my arms, but I am not going to question it now. Subtly, I tilt my head down to sniff her black curls. She smells of the fresh cut greenery of the Meadows and the sweet scent of open air.

"Thank you, Meshi," she whispers after a while. "I know this is probably...really fucking weird for you, but I really needed a hug...and a friend."

"Well, you can always come to me for either of those things."

I would be her friend for now, and hopefully one day, much more.

14

Hope

Listen, this is not how I would feel if I were hugging a friend. I thought it'd be awkward, what with the wings, but now that I'm wrapped in his leathery embrace, all I can focus on is Meshi. I'm so warm and cozy, enveloped in his wing, with my head tucked against his chest, I could fall asleep, except for the fact that I am extremely aware of his bare skin so close to mine. It must be because most everyone here wears these long-sleeved jumpsuits, so I'm not used to it anymore, but I'm suddenly picturing *his* jumpsuit, with the sleeves cut off to accommodate his wings, and the beefy bicep that is right next to my head right now.

My body goes hot all over. *Too* hot. I'm aware of every single point of contact between the two of us. I'm also, not for the first time, disparaging these stupid, standard-issue jumpsuits for their full-body coverage.

Alright, Hope, that is quite enough of that. While I give myself a mental talking-to, I gently extricate myself from Meshi's comforting embrace. He releases me immediately and I scramble to my feet before turning around. Meshi stretches his legs in front of himself casually but doesn't make to stand, so I stand over him awkwardly trying to find something to say.

My first inclination is to say something rude, to make him feel as uncomfortable as I suddenly do. His eyes are kind, though. His lips turn up in an easy smile. I can't bring myself to say something that might wipe it away.

"So, uh, thanks. For this..." I gesture vaguely between us. "Anyways, I gotta go. Night!"

I turn tail to run, but Meshi speaks up before I manage a step.

"Good night, Hope. I'll message you on your data pad to let you know when we can meet up and work on our project," his smooth timbre informs me.

I nod without looking, afraid I will sit back down if I do, and speed-walk around the corner. Once I'm a few yards down the adjacent corridor I pick up speed, running the rest of the way home.

The apartment was quiet when I came in last night. This morning, I stare at the ceiling and listen for sounds, proof that Prue and possibly even Asper stayed here last night. I can't hear anything, but I can't bear to get up yet, not with the possibility of facing my sister and her girlfriend in their pajamas, small as it may be. I'm going to have to apologize to them at some point. Should I do it in my pajamas? The entire train of thought makes me prickly all over.

After a while my bladder forces me to get up, and I've waited so long that I don't even grab my jumpsuit, just dash out to the bathroom across the hall. Once I've relieved myself, I figure I should bite the bullet, so I head for the kitchen in search of Prue, holey pajamas and all.

The automatic lights follow me through the apartment, into the kitchen, where our Originem-assigned data pad lays out on the counter. A light blinks in the corner and I eye it warily.

Prue knows I hate technology. I was a complete dunce with cell phones and computers back home, and I'm no better with alien technology. Spoiler alert, I'm actually worse. After accidentally bricking a few of these datapads back on the satellite station, Prue and I agreed that she would handle anything that required doing on the datapads. That's how she got us signed up for this space station civilization without me ever knowing. Until she woke me up one morning and told me we'd been accepted, anyway.

Gathering up my courage, I lean forward on the balls of my feet, the chrome floor cold against my bare skin, and tap on the black screen. It lights up immediately and I jump a little. The screen is a confusing mess of little icons that I don't recognize, but one, that kind of looks like a ladybug without the face, has a blinking red dot on it, so I take a chance and tap it.

Lines of English come across the screen and I realize this is like texting. The top line is flashing, Prue's name bold across the top. I'm quite proud of myself as I read her message about getting her own wristpad and staying at Asper's. She doesn't mention our argument, but she doesn't mention the fact that I am even accessing this message either. She should be so proud of me! She's definitely still mad.

Not that I blame her. It kind of sucks. I want to be done with it. Apologize to Prue and Asper and move on with our lives. They have a baby to worry about, after all.

I somehow manage to get back to the main messaging screen after typing Prue a hasty reply, but there are no other new messages. No requests to meetup from a certain tall, winged male. Not that I'm looking for any.

This day is *not* starting off on the right foot. I need a distraction.

The petals I pilfered off Bazzel last night are still in the pockets of my jumpsuit, a little crushed, but fine for what I'll be using them for. It's been a while since I made my own dye, but the process is simple enough. I got three indigo petals and two fuschia ones, all as big as my palm or larger. After a moment's consideration, I toss all five in one of our kitchen bowls then muddle them into a paste with a fork.

It takes a little more time to figure out how to get hot water from the nutritional printer—and then take a short coffee break since I had extra hot water and Prue graciously left some coffee behind—but soon I'm letting my soon-to-be homemade paint steep in steaming water and I'm realizing that this project has...a lot of waiting.

Two hours in a barebones apartment with few worldly possessions is a very, *very* long time. Somehow I survive though and the payoff is... *So. Good.* The fuschia and indigo have fused to make a bright, flashy violet and I can't stop staring at how vibrant it is.

Now for the second problem. No paper. No blank canvas to cast my art upon. I lay my jumpsuit out on to the counter lovingly, tucking the collar in.

This thing is probably the only reason I didn't turn into a full on hussy last night.

Perhaps there is some merit to the full-body coverage. The plain gray, though, I can no longer allow. Between the collar and the breast pocket I use my fingerprints to make a chain of violet flowers. They're crude and the color doesn't penetrate the fabric as much as I'd like, but they add a pop of brightness to our otherwise drab uniform.

Now, if I could find some bleach and collect more petals, I could really make something magical happen here.

Excited to show off my new project, I jump in a shower while my new pattern dries, taking the time to wash and condition my unruly curls. At least that's one thing the Originem got right. When we moved into the apartment, it was already stocked with hair products that actually went with my hair texture, and different products for Prue's straight, shiny hair. Mine smells like eucalyptus and leaves my usually uncontrollable bob in pretty, wavy curls.

Before too long I'm stepping out of the apartment and into the corridor. Destiny mentioned a market on division five, but I'm not even sure how to get to the elevators, so I meander around the public spaces, content to smile and nod at passing citizens. It feels very *Pleasantville* but it isn't entirely *un*pleasant either. Almost like I belong here.

Pretty much everyone wears the standard grey jumpsuits but every so often I see someone in what I am going to assume is traditional attire from their home planet. When a periwinkle Silfan walks by dressed like a punk from the London scene, I almost gasp. Bazzel will have to help me connect with them at some point. I need to get my hands on some of those silver spikes.

A familiar form comes into view, towering over the rest of the crowd and dampening my mood immediately.

The Originem don't tend to mingle among station citizens much, I've noticed. So seeing Lokas casually walking down the hall, chatting with a sandy blonde Dhugaren woman, is a bit disconcerting. I'm trying to be more optimistic, more open to the possibility that everything here can be taken at face value. All of that goes out the window when I see the tall, slender Originem coming towards me. I don't know why they freak me out, but I can't stop the cold that trickles down my spine. I start to turn around, but it's already too late.

"Hope! Hello!" Lokas shouts from ten yards away, waving his long arm at me. The double-joints hinge grotesquely and I fight the urge to flee.

The Orginem *saved* us. They are good aliens. It's wrong to keep villainizing them because of their appearance. It's downright *racist*, Hope! I sternly tell myself, before forcing a smile onto my face.

"Hi Lokas," I call out as he and his companion approach. "How are you doing?"

"Quite well, thank you. Let me introduce you to my friend, Brogg." He gestured to the Dhugaren woman at his side, who nods at me with a toothy grin.

"Well met, Hope. I love what you've done with your jumpsuit. What did you use?" she asks me, her deep, guttural voice deeper than most human men.

"I made a dye from the culled flowers in the Silfan Meadows," I told her proudly, puffing my chest up a bit so she can see it better. Glancing at Lokas, I quickly tack on, "they're free for anyone to take."

"Now, that's the Sanctuary spirit!" Lokas proclaims cheerfully. "I knew you had it in you."

I'm starting to feel like a kid the way I am having to crane my neck up at these two very tall aliens, but I manage to keep the petulance out of my tone when I ask, "what does that mean, Lokas?"

"Community, sustainability, and innovation!" Brogg growls cheerfully. "The Originem's three favorite words, especially this one."

She points a claw towards the Originem in question so casually, I almost keel over. I guess I wouldn't be afraid of much either if I was over six foot tall with sharp claws. Lucky.

"Well, I do love to see the creative and *innovative* ways station citizens find to circumvent their limitations," he chuckles.

"I sure wish you'd shared that tidbit when you visited me last week," I grumble.

I'm starting to catch on to this place a bit more.

"You didn't give us any resources, any support. Humans need support systems, you can't just toss them in the water and tell them to swim," I huff. I can feel my blood starting to heat up. The Originem set us up for failure basically.

"Ah-ha!" Brogg guffaws, slapping her thigh. "That's how we Dhugarens teach our cubs how to swim, too."

"That is *not* how we teach our kids to swim," I mutter. I mean, that's how some people did it, but that's not how I would do it. Explaining that would dilute my argument, so instead, I pivot. "Humans need support systems, other people they can talk about their problems and share resources with."

"That's a brilliant idea, Hope!" Lokas cries and I look at him in bewilderment.

"What is?" I ask, confused. I'm gearing up for an argument that does not seem to be coming.

"A support group for humans," he replies, looking at me like I'm a bit stupid.

Maybe I am, because no matter how many times I'm proven wrong about this station and its citizens, I am as befuddled as the last time. Perhaps it's time I stop thinking the absolute worst of this place and its Originem creators and start thinking about how I can be a part of it instead.

"Where would I even start? I can barely check the messages on our data pad." I will run through these corridors with handmade flyers if I have to, but alas, no paper, and no clue where the elevators are. I should probably figure that part out first.

"I will send you a directory of all the humans here so you can message them. In the meantime, you should ask your neighbors for help." His tone turns admonishing, "Your sister has integrated quite well here. She's already familiar with one of the most reclusive races on the station. You should take a page from her book, as you humans say."

While Lokas and Brogg chortle together at humans' apparently ridiculous turn of phrases, I fight not to roll my eyes all the way into the back of my head. This guy is *not* invited to the support group...though guests speakers from other races would be a great idea... Mind whirling with possibilities, I say goodbye to Lokas and Brogg and practically run back to my apartment. Grabbing my data pad I take off again for the Meadows, the only place I know how to get to, and the most likely place to find a friend.

15

Meshi

When Khur first started courting Destiny, our Originem supervisor, Josep, told us that humans thought 'absence makes the heart grow fonder.' Destiny did *not* agree with this, and was quite upset with Khur for 'ghosting' her for a few days. I'm starting to see that my Hope is nothing like Khur's Destiny, though. I think a little space may be exactly what she needs.

It doesn't make it any easier to stay away from her, though. Not when my mind is full of abyss black curls and the floral scent she carries with her. Which is exactly why I find myself in the maintenance office, sorting through old maintenance requests and marking most of them resolved. Khur is a bit of a workaholic, or he was before he met Destiny, anyways. He would jump up and run to resolve the issue the moment a ticket hit our queue. That's why I am often on other floors, helping with maintenance and mechanical repairs. Khur isn't very good at paperwork, though. I don't mind spending a little extra time helping him close out his tickets. It's the least I can do.

Imagine my surprise when the corner of my data pad lights up, indicating I have a new message, and what comes up on the screen isn't a name, but the Winged-One's word for *hope*. That feeling is exactly what rises in my chest as I tap a claw gently on the message and read what she has to say.

I bet you didn't expect me to message you first, did you, Wings? Well, neither did I, but I need your help with something. Meet me at the Meadows right before the lights dim tonight.

My feet, previously resting on the corner of my desk, hit the chrome floor with a thud. The pounding of my heavy work boots reverberate around the office as I stomp towards the door, before turning and stomping right back.

It's just after lunch time. Not a few, but several hours lie between now and the dimming of the lights on the station. Lowering myself back behind my desk, I pick up my data pad but stare at it blankly, unseeing.

"Something I can help you with, friend?" Josep's calm voice jolts me out of my daydreaming and I almost jump in my seat. I've forgotten he is here.

"How do you know so much about human courting rituals, Josep?" I ask him, trying to distract myself.

"I lived on Earth—that's what they call their home planet—for a while, before I was stationed here." He sounds sad, though I can't imagine why. He's been here as long as I have...

"But that would be over twenty years ago..." I do some quick math. "How old are you, Josep?"

"This will be my seventy second year." He explains, "Originem age much slower than our descendants. It's one of our main differences."

Years I'd worked with this male, and I would never have guessed him that much older than myself. He still has a youthful, line-free face, and moves with the grace and vitality of a young man.

"What are the other differences?" I ask, feeling guilty that I've never thought to ask my colleague more about himself.

Josep is always kind and supportive of Khur's and my own endeavors, never asks anything of us, actually, except the one time he asked Khur to go to therapy. The Originem have positioned themselves into places of benevolent, albeit distant, authority, and for the first time I recognize the invisible line that separates us.

"We struggle to reproduce. There are maybe a dozen Originem children born every year. Originem males have a very high sterility rate, so it is common for our women to take several husbands, to increase her chances of conceiving. The numbers dwindle every year, though."

"Is that what happens when you get promoted? You get sent upstairs and paired with a wife?" It is common knowledge that Originem who are promoted in their positions are sent to the top division of Sanctuary Station, where the administration offices are. There, they don't have to integrate with the other citizens like they do on the rest of the divisions.

It's actually always rubbed me the wrong way—like being segregated away from the rest of us aliens is a reward to them, which is so counterintuitive to their entire message here. If that is the case, though, that their reward is the chance to start a family, I can understand the desire.

"No. I have no desire for an Originem wife," he admits. "But I believe you were going to ask me about the humans. Did you find one you're fond of as well?"

"I did," I confess. "I wonder, though, why haven't there been any interspecies couples before now? Do you believe it's taboo?"

"No, not at all," he confides. "In fact, I think that the administration would be very pleased to see the community integrated in such a way. We have noticed humans are a bit more adventurous than other descendants. Maybe they were invited here to finally break that barrier."

I ponder this for a moment. I don't know how I feel about the fact that Josep practically admitted that humans were brought to Sanctuary Station to mingle. On one hand, it's thrilling to consider Hope, *adventurous* Hope, breaking barriers with *me*. On the other hand, the thought of the Originem inviting Hope, Destiny, Prue and all those other women here for that specific reason sends a frisson of unease down my spine.

"Josep, what is the purpose of this place?" I ask, for the first time in my life. I've never questioned my home until now.

"Sanctuary Station is just that. A sanctuary for all of our descendants who deserve a fresh start, a new home." He pauses, leveling me with a heavy look. "It is also an experiment in many ways—one that I assure you has a singular outcome in mind, to create a better world for everyone."

I nod my head, not bothering to reply out loud. I trust the Originem, and even if I didn't, I have nowhere else to go. We're all here to make the best of the circumstances we've been presented with. Sometimes, that's the best we can do.

The lights dim as I walk through the automatic doors and into the Meadows, casting the rolling fields in a soft blue glow. Hope is here, perched on one of the long benches against the wall of the biome, clutching her data pad tightly against her chest.

She looks...vulnerable. She's obviously much shorter than I am, but I've never seen her as *small* until this moment. She always seems so fiery, so full of life. All those times, even last night when she cried on my chest, I wanted nothing more than to worship her, to lay on the ground so she may have a pedestal on which to stand when she inevitably takes over the entire station. Today, though, as I stare at her and see her from a different light, I get the urge to wrap my wings around her and shelter her from the rest of the world. Hope always puts on a tough image, but I see through that, now more than ever.

I see the oversized heart she tries to hide behind her anger.

It's easy to stick to the shadows in the dimly lit biome. She doesn't see me until I am settling onto the bench next to her, and then she starts as if jarred from a deep thought.

"Meshi. You came," she breathes, glancing quickly at me then back towards the open space of the Silfan Meadows spread out before us.

"What can I do for you, Hope?"

"I need—" She takes a deep breath, as if preparing for a big leap. "—help."

She laughs, little bells of joy that make my wings tingle. "That wasn't as hard as I expected. Okay." She finally turns her face towards me, her shoulders losing some of their strain. “I need to learn how to be a better citizen here. I wanted to send you a message and it took me over an hour and I ended up having to ask my neighbor for help.” She hisses the last part through clenched teeth, then glances away quickly. “It’s hard for me to ask for help. I’m working on that.”

“We can go over some basics on your datapad,” I immediately agree, knowing better than to address the other part. She is similar to my older brother, Shemo, in that way. Stubborn as stalactites, as Ma says anytime he gets on about something. For a while, it was Furga, but we’re all relieved *that* particular saga has finally ended peacefully. They’re taking it slow, so they say, but there’s no doubt in anyone’s mind they’re gonna be married before the end of the rotation. I’m actually surprised Maklash hasn’t started taking bets on the announcement yet.

“It’s not just that. It’s everything. I couldn’t even find the elevators earlier today. I had no idea how to leave this division. What if there’s a fire?” she exclaims. “Is that even something I should be worried about? Or should I be worried about meteors instead?”

Her dark eyes look a little wild, black eyebrows arching high on her forehead. I run the back of my claws against the ridges there, careful to keep the tips pointed away. It is a cool, calming sensation, one my mother uses on all of us when we are upset. It seems to work for Hope, too, her pale, expressive face turning into one of sweet hesitation. Her jaw is warm and delicate when I cup it in my hand.

“Why did you choose to ask me for help, of all people?” I ask, leaning over her and putting my wing around her shoulder.

“I guess...I knew you wouldn’t judge me or make fun of me. And I knew you wouldn’t say no.” She smiles up at me bashfully, but I’m not offended. She's right on both accounts. I would never say no to her, and honestly, asking for help when you need it is always an admirable move.

I'm not thinking very admirable thoughts right now, though. I've drawn her closer to me as we spoke, and, leaning over her like I am, our faces are mere inches apart. I know of the human custom of kissing. Winged-Ones do it, too, though much more rarely from what I gather. I want to sink into the plush, pink lips before me, explore her small, plump mouth, the tongue I've seen peeking out at me every time she says something fierce and biting. I want Hope to want it as much as I do, though, and I'm not sure we are quite there, yet.

"Come with me." I stand up quickly, pulling her with me. She giggles, but follows, allowing me to extract her datapad from her grip and put it in my workbag. "I'm going to show you how to get to the elevators, so pay attention."

"To the elevators? Now?" She keeps hold of my claw, careful to grip near my palm, as we rush towards the corridor.

"Hope, I am going to show you my people's biome tonight."

16

Hope

Meshi giving instructions is surprisingly serious. He stops at each corridor, pointing out the digital screens showing flashing green numbers in different languages near the top. We wait for the Arabic number to show up while he explains that most divisions are set up this way, with the numbers making a grid-like pattern on each level. He takes the time to explain some things I should have definitely been told when I got here. Apparently there's a lot in the orientation videos Prue didn't think to share with me.

I don't mention that, though, when he takes the time to explain that there's a supply station every ten floors. Normally, I would go to the supply station on division fifteen, which covers divisions eleven through twenty. He tells me, though, that Destiny has a fulfillment position at the one on division five, where her apartment is, along with Meshi's and Khur's.

That's what they call *jobs* here...fulfillment positions. Everyone here gets a living wage in the stations credits, and our nutritional printers are always stocked, but if you get a *fulfillment position* you can make extra credits for luxuries. It's still a *job* no matter how pretty you paint it up.

I don't say all of this as Meshi explains that the Winged-One biome is not in the same division he lives in. He shows me how to lock the elevator in place while we wait on the digital number pad to change to familiar characters, mentioning how lucky it is we all have number systems based on ten. I didn't even know that.

I'm trying not to let it get to me, but I'm starting to get a little annoyed at everything Prue hasn't told me about this place.

As soon as the elevator starts moving, Meshi turns me around by my shoulders, peering at my chest.

"I thought something was different, but I couldn't quite tell in the dimmed lights," he murmurs, pulling my collar up to stretch the fabric flat. "This is lovely, Hope. Did you use flowers from the Meadows?"

My heart gives a funny little thump at his recognition, both in seeing my new decoration at all, and at him realizing what I may have used as a medium. My chin tilts up to meet his gaze and his knuckles barely graze my neck, but I swear I can feel it all over my body and my nipples tighten in sweet anticipation as he leans towards me, dark eyes keeping me motionless except to press up ever so slightly on my toes to meet him.

The elevator dings, the doors sliding open with a swish, and Meshi is leaving my personal space—thank goodness, that's the second time we almost kissed! He holds out a wing, claws open invitingly. Placing my fingers into the soft palm in the center and allowing him to lead me into another, nondescript, dimly lit division corridor, I feel a familiar rush low in my belly that I'm afraid to name, a kaleidoscope of butterflies I am not prepared for or expecting. I think...if the situation were to arise again, you know, naturally...I think I do want Meshi to kiss me.

"See how much taller the ceiling is here? I know it's kind of dark, but can you see the ledge there, about ten feet up?" He points into the darkness above us and I see vague shadows.

"Kind of," I answer him, "and doors along the ledges, right? Are those individual apartments?"

"Well, not here in the main corridor, no. They open into smaller ones just like these doors," he gestures along the wall next to us, where doors lead into individual subdivisions every thirty yards or so.

"How do other citizens visit you? Or, like what if someone is sick or elderly?" This system seems extremely flawed.

"We have smaller elevators we can access in the lower subdivisions." His grin makes his fangs push into his lower lip, but instead of making him look ferocious, he looks almost boyish. "It's sweet of you to think of the less fortunate Winged-Ones on Sanctuary. My ma has a hard time flying sometimes, and she takes the elevators. I'm sure she'd love some company if you ever want to see."

Oh, Heaven help me, was Meshi also a mama's boy? How did I ever think I would be able to resist when the Originem assigned me an alien seducer. One thing I'm certain of, though, is that if that's what *is* happening here, then Meshi is as in the dark as I am. There's just no way he could be anything but the sweet, somewhat oblivious but still unbelievably capable male that is currently tugging me down a shadowy corridor to show me his race's biome.

"It's just around the corner here. We'll remember to check the coordinates of this intersection when we leave," he declares. "I don't want to wait now."

Laughing unselfconsciously now, I follow him at a jog on my much-shorter legs, letting his enthusiasm infect me as we approach a pair of familiar looking automatic doors. Before we pass through he pauses, tugging me close to him. I let him.

"It's even darker in there," he nods towards the doors. "There are *nifir* lining the primary caverns and tunnels, but much of the Caverns are pitch black."

"How can you see? Is your eyesight that much better?"

"No, actually, it's only marginally better than other descendent species. It's our sonar sense that gives us the unfair advantage down here." I'm glad we're still out here where I can see some things, like the smirk he tosses towards me like an air-kiss. My stomach does flip flops.

It's official. I have absolutely lost my mind. At least I'm not the only one. Prue and Destiny are right there with me. Hell, most of the women who moved here probably are. Humans really are a bunch of freaks.

"Well, you can have your unfair advantage as long as you use it to find me if I get lost in the dark."

"You don't even have to ask."

The male with wings and claws and fangs leads me into the dark. It's the most excited I've been in ages.

Lining either side of the cavern are clumps of *nifir*, a glowing crystal Meshi told me about. He follows the path they illuminate with confidence, pulling me close to whisper in my ear as we go. My arms prickle with goosebumps.

"My people lived underground on my home planet, in these vast cave systems that spanned entire nations, from what I was told."

"Were you born on the station?"

"I was just a kit when we came to live here. I don't remember it, but my ma says the Originem led an entire nation of people into the sunlight for the first time in centuries." His eyes get that faraway look in them for a moment before he smiles at me, shaking it off.

"Centuries? Why? What kind of environmental disaster makes you stay in a cave for centuries?"

"Our planet wasn't destroyed, Hope." His pause is extended, pregnant. "There are two sentient species on Bejkarr. The Winged-Ones, and the Nosferation. They look very similar to us, except instead of wings, they have arms."

"No way! I haven't seen any of them here."

"No, you wouldn't. There was a war centuries ago, and the Winged-Ones lost. We've been forced underground since then, treated like chattel and vermin. Even hunted for sport, at times."

"Meshi, that's terrible. I had no idea." I sputter. "I mean, I thought everyone was here because their planets were destroyed by global warming or something."

"No, not all of us." He squeezes my hand. "That is why you call us Winged-Ones, though. Because that is the Nosferation word for my kind. It translates directly into *Winged-Ones.*"

"Wait, so we're all basically calling you a slur when we say that?" I exclaim, appalled.

"What? No. It's simply an observation. And an accurate one, even here. We're the only race I've seen with wings."

"I... I guess." It still didn't feel right to me.

"Come on, there's something I want to show you."

He tugs me down one of the unlit offshoot tunnels, never letting go of my hand. His palm is warm and the points of his claws press ever so slightly into the back of my hand. It doesn't hurt, it lets me know *exactly* whose hand I'm holding. It's a comforting tether as we leave what little light the *nifir* provides behind us.

"Just around the corner here," Meshi whispers.

"This better be good," I whisper back, only half-joking.

I wasn't *scared* of the dark, but anyone would be uncomfortable walking through the pitch black like this. The only reason I'm not freaking out right now is because Meshi's hand is warm and soft, and because I know he's using his sonar sense to watch over me. It's obvious he has had a crush on me for a while now. At first, it was annoying. All I could see was an alien casanova sent by the Originem to seduce me into complacence. I know that sounds crazy, but it certainly seemed more likely than the truth. Why would the Originem do this? Take care of all these different beings? It seemed more likely that Meshi was part of some larger web of conspiracy.

Now that I've seen more of him, though, I can see how foolish that is. He's so genuine, so earnest, and after the last year plus of my life, I really appreciate anything I can take at face-value. Maybe that's why I've had such a hard time accepting this space station as well, because for so long, nothing was as it seemed, and now that the world might be a (somewhat) reliable place again, it feels too good to be true.

When Meshi guides me around yet another dark corner and into a cavern, I have to blink a few times before my eyes adjust. I'm not quite sure what I'm seeing, but the view before me is beautiful. The room glows faintly, barely illuminated enough to see shapes and shadows. The light emanates from clusters of crystals that grow all across the room, getting progressively bigger the further in I look. Closer to the entrance, the crystals are smaller, no taller than my ankles, jagged little green things like cacti with their sharp-looking points. Several yards away, near the far wall of the massive cavern, the crystals look like they could be as big as my entire person, maybe taller. Rows are carved between them all, cleared paths lined with round, grey stones. The stones turn into prisms of color next to the sparkling, glowing *nifir* that seem to grow right out of the ground here.

I stand for several seconds, clutching Meshi's palm and taking in the incredible sight in front of me, before I remember how to speak again.

"I didn't realize there were such beautiful things on this space station."

I blink and am surprised to feel tears welling in my eyes, blurring my vision. I turn to the male by my side. His dark eyes reflect the colorful glow that surrounds us.

"What is this place?" I whisper.

"This is our crystal garden. Most of these are descended from transplants from our home planet." Even in the dark, I can see the pride shining on his face clearly.

"You grow them? How? Don't they take, like, thousands of years to form?" I have a feeling that is an incredibly low guesstimate.

"Not these crystals. They're special," he explains. "They're sacred to my people. We use them for special gifts and rituals...That's actually why I wanted to bring you here. I mentioned it the other day, but...A traditional gift for pregnant women is a *minkla*, with crystals of various colors and cuts, to reflect and stain the lights different hues against their walls. It entertains the kits and soothes them to have something pretty to look at."

His smile is shy and I realize that he is waiting for my approval.

"Meshi, that's a lovely gift," I tell him, "and it means a lot that you would ask me to help with it. Maybe we could include some pressed flowers from the Meadows."

"That's a great idea! We could include different things from different biomes, maybe? To represent our blended community."

"Meshi, I think we could make a great team," I exclaim, full of ideas. It's been so long since I've gotten to really stretch my creative muscles, it seems I forgot how for a moment. This, though...this is exactly what I need. I step closer to him, relishing the heat of his body as I place his claw onto my shoulder and place my hand on his chest.

"I agree," Meshi swallows, his nerves obvious in his shaking voice. "That's why...that's why I'd like to court you, Hope. Maybe not in the human way, or the Winged-One way, but in our own way."

He brings his other wing around me, so I am enclosed in his dark embrace. My hands rest—finally—on those beefy shoulders and I can't help but rub them down to his biceps and give them a little squeeze. Let me tell you, they are hard as rocks. Meshi's breath shakes as he awaits my answer, his nervousness so endearing and guileless, any thoughts of him being an Originem spy wither and die. I tilt my chin up and tell him what I really want.

"Kiss me, Meshi."

As he leans down to meet me, I keep my eyes open, entranced by the green reflected in his black gaze. His lips are warm and soft, and though he keeps the kiss chaste with his mouth firmly closed, I feel it all the way to my toes.

He retreats all too quickly and I grab his face, pulling him back down and pressing my lips more firmly to his. Meshi makes a sound of surprise, but quickly wraps his wings around my back, pulling me closer as well. Our mouths part in synchrony and his long, narrow tongue pushes into my mouth. The feeling is absolutely alien and utterly *obscene* as he takes over, tasting every inch of the inside of my mouth with that extremely flexible muscle of his.

By the time we part, several minutes later, I'm panting like I've run a marathon. I'm absolutely ready to strip off these jumpsuits and make the beast with two backs right the fuck now. I reach for the zipper hiding Meshi's chest from me—he definitely has pecs, I can tell—and he withdraws a claw from around me to catch my hands.

"What's your problem? Do you not want...?" I refuse to voice it out loud. No way am I throwing myself at this guy for him to turn me down.

"I do want...I want very, very much, but I think we should take things slowly." Meshi's voice is pained and his claw squeezes my hand ever so slightly. "I want to court you. I want to prove myself to you, so that when we do copulate, you will know that there will be no one else for you ever again. Only me."

My knees threaten to buckle at his bold assertion, even if it is accompanied by some old-fashioned ideas. The lust it ignites in my veins—and my pussy—is warring with the fear and hesitation his words spur in me. I am not looking for some big commitment. I just like his muscly arms. And his kind, caring nature. And his thoughtfulness has given me a gift I have been yearning for.

Dammit.

"Fine. You can court me while we make this baby mobile thing. I'm going to need help figuring out how to organize a human support group, anyways. That's one of the reasons I need you to teach me how to be a good citizen here," I catch myself rambling. "You can court me while we do all those things."

Meshi nods enthusiastically in response, the top fangs peeking out of his contagious smile reflecting the glowing crystals. "That sounds perfect, my Hope."

17

Hope

After that evening in the Winged-One biome, everything starts to get a bit easier, a bit brighter. I could say that it's because of how quickly my life has filled back up with art. Between the children's many suggestions for different mediums, most of which Meshi helped me identify, and my almost daily meetings with Meshi designing our mobile, I am almost embarrassed at how I acted when I first arrived on Sanctuary Station.

I could say it's the art, but it would be a partial lie.

It's not *just* the art.

It's the sweet, caring, resourceful, reliable alien who's somehow wormed his way into the daily fabric of my life. It's like as soon as I agreed to let him court me, he threw out any illusion of casualness, not that he was ever giving casual vibes to begin with.

I want to push him away, to deny the crazy sparks between us, but for the last two weeks, he's shown up at my door almost every day, and when he doesn't he always tells me the day before. He asks how I'm doing, then he *listens* when I answer. One day I joked that I would kill for some chocolate and he showed up the next day with a Mercasian dessert that tasted like chocolate pudding. How can I resist a guy who brings me chocolate pudding?

In short, Meshi is making it very hard to resist him and I'm really starting to lose sight of why I wanted to in the first place. The biggest complaint I have now is that when he said he wanted to take things slow he meant it. The worst part is, he makes no effort to hide how much he wants me, always touching me with the back of his claws or tucking a wing around my shoulders. It sets my blood on fire every time, and though he always kisses me, passionately, for several minutes, before we part ways, he hasn't made a move to take it any further yet, and I refuse to try again after being rejected so soundly last time.

My pride can only take so much.

Apparently, my wrist can only take so much, as well, though, because I swear I'm starting to get carpal tunnel from the amount of manual masturbation I'm having to do. If I could go back to Earth and grab one thing, well, I think at this point it would be a vibrator.

Which is why I've decided, after nearly two weeks of "courting" that I'm making my move today, pride be damned. If Meshi rejects me again, I'll have to find one of those airlocks to push myself out of, but hopefully it won't come to that.

When the doorbell in my apartment chimes, I am already waiting to let him in. His tranquil, confident smile disarms me every time, knocking my defenses down with a peek of those sharp fangs. He's always so careful when he's kissing me, so gentle when he touches me, that it's impossible to see him as scary, even with the sharp fangs and claws. I know he would never hurt me.

That smile makes me fumble, but I recover quickly and pull him in my apartment by the collar of his jumpsuit. He comes willingly, the door swishing closed behind him. When my legs hit the back of the couch, I pull him down over top of me and bring my face up to meet his. Our mouths clash together messily and I barely avoid cutting a lip on one of those aforementioned fangs, but we find our rhythm soon. His claws grasp the arm of the couch above my head and my hands are trapped between us, along with his workbag slung around his hips. I'm so glad to finally feel any part of his large body against my own, that it's easy to ignore the sharp angles of his tools digging into my hip.

Our tongues tangle together, his overpowering my own in the most delicious way. When we finally break apart we're both breathing heavily.

"Hi," I squeak out awkwardly as Meshi peers down at me with heat in his gaze.

"Hello, my Hope," he murmurs, his deep voice vibrating my chest.

That's what he's called me since that day in the Caves, too. *His* Hope. I don't want to acknowledge the embers it ignites deep inside me every time I hear it. He's staked his claim in every way except the one that I really want.

"Part of human courting," I start the speech I'd put together this morning, "is being physically intimate with each other, getting to know each other's bodies. We don't have to go all the way, but you know, we could do more than kiss."

I try to grind my pelvis up against him, but the workbag gets in the way a bit. Which is right about when the awkwardness starts to creep in, as I become more aware of my supine position, how my arms are crushed between our chests, and the way he's looking down at me with resistance in his eyes.

Before he can reject me again and send me on a self-pity spiral that ends in the vacuum of space, I push hard against his chest with my trapped arms.

"Dont. Don't say it. I don't understand why you keep leading me on like this if you don't want me." I push harder when he doesn't budge. "Get the fuck off me, dude."

Meshi moves away, rising to his feet, and something sharp stabs me in the chest. Scrambling up to sit, I push my back against the couch and pull my knees to my chest like a shield. He watches me, his expression guarded, and it pisses me off.

"Just get out. I don't want to play these games with you anymore." I turn my head away, willing the angry tears pooling in my waterline not to fall.

"My sweet, beautiful Hope," Meshi says, "I promise you, I am not playing games."

I keep my head turned, pressing my chin into my shoulder, and nodding slightly. I am *not* a weeper, and I'm mortified that I'm doing it a second time in this idiot's presence.

"Look at me." His voice is stern, his tone sharper than I've ever heard it. My neck moves before my brain catches up, my watery eyes meeting his intense black ones.

"I wanted to take things slow so you would know you can trust me, so you know this is not just physical for me." As he speaks he reaches for his workbag, unbuckling it and letting it clatter to the ground. "I never meant for you to feel unwanted by me. You're the only thing I've ever wanted." He reaches up and tugs down the zipper lining his chest. "I told myself I would let you take the lead when I first saw you, and if you are taking the lead now, I will gladly follow." He unhooks buttons I hadn't seen hidden along his shoulders with deft claws and the top half of his worksuit falls, bunching at his waist.

Horny Hope has completely taken over my lizard brain at this point, because the tears have dried right up—or maybe migrated south a little. He *does* have pecs, and under them a whole stack of ab muscles. Framing them in a perfect V are those muscles Olympic swimmers have. I have no clue what they are called but I bet they'd feel so good pushed up against me. I wipe the side of my mouth in case there's drool.

He kneels on the floor in front of me, our height differences so vast that we're almost eye-to-eye now, and gently pulls my arms down from where they're wrapped around my leg-shield. Next, he wraps his claws around my calves, letting them prick me a bit. Meshi is usually so careful with them that I know this must be purposeful. The danger that lurks beneath the surface, but somehow doesn't exist at all with this male, intoxicates me as he pulls my legs forward, putting one on either side of his kneeling figure.

He runs his palms up my thighs to my hips, which he uses to pull me to the edge of the couch. Letting out an undignified squeal, I reach for his shoulders for balance. When we're this close, eye-to-eye like this, our breaths mingling together, it's so easy for me to let the rest of the world fall away, to forget that he's an alien and I'm also an alien here on this space station in the sky, lightyears away from Earth. It's easy to forget that my entire life has been upended and I've been thrust into an especially altruistic episode of Star Trek that will inevitably reveal a terrible twist moments before the credits roll.

Here with Meshi I could almost believe there won't be a twist.

Meshi makes no move to take this further, just grips me by my love handles, one claw on each hand pressing into the tops of my asscheeks. In this position, I can do what I've been secretly wanting to do for weeks now. I run my hands from his shoulders, up the sides of his neck, lightly scraping my fingernails against his smooth scalp, before finding those velvety-soft looking ears of his.

I've been eyeballing these babies since that night in the caves, and all my predictions were right. They're soft as satin, cool to the touch and delicate as petals. I rub them gently between the pads of my fingers and watch Meshi's dark eyes become instantly hooded. I had a feeling they were erogenous; looks like I may be right.

Keeping my eyes locked on his, I lean forward and press a wet, sensual kiss to his eager lips, invading his open mouth with my tongue. It is no match for his much longer one, but he lets me control the kiss anyway, tilting his head back slightly to give me better access.

A ragged moan escapes him when I give his ears a light tug, putting a little bit of bite in it with my fingernails. His palms are kneading my ass cheeks, claws pricking ever so slightly, and the liquid heat pooling in my belly is growing by the second. When I break the kiss, Meshi's lips follow mine desperately. His hunger stokes my own higher and with a firm shove on his shoulders, I push him onto his back on the floor of my living room.

Leaning back on the elbow joints of his wings, Meshi watches me slip off the couch and land on my hands and knees between his outstretched legs. He watches as I stalk towards him, a predator who's found her prey, and he bites his lip with one white fang. I want to lick every part of him, from those sensitive ears, across those beefy biceps, down the V that leads me straight to the bulge making itself known between his legs, and down his inner thigh, and—*holy shit* does this guy have a Louisville Slugger between his legs? Whatever the fuck I'm looking at is almost down to his damn knees! I'm so stunned I freeze, like a complete idiot, and stare at this bulge—is it his cock? It seems seems presumptuous at this point—wondering what the *fuck* I am going to do with that.

"We knew there would be...differences in our bodies," Meshi stutters.

"Differences?" I choke out. "Are Winged-One females hollow inside?"

"No," he mutters and belatedly, I realize he's flustered. "Winged-Ones evolved to copulate in the air, while flying. There are ways," he gestures to the sapling growing between his legs, "to make this work between us."

Taking a moment to really look at him, I'm forced to realize I may have hurt his feelings. Our bodies *are* different. It's so obvious, yet somehow I expected him to look a certain way under his clothes, which is completely ridiculous. Not once has Meshi looked at me like I'm strange or distasteful, and while there is maybe a little *unease* at the thought of trying to fit whatever that is inside my pussy, it's certainly not aversion. Keeping my eyes locked on his face, I start crawling towards him again, pushing his legs together and straddling his thighs. My hands find purchase against the hard muscles of his abdomen.

His cock—I'm ready to admit, that's probably his cock—presses insistently up against my ass and if I angle my hips just right and lower my body towards his...I push his chest until he's laying flat back and find the angle I was hoping for.

The doubt still lingers on his gentle expression, so I cant my hips and press into his bulge, whispering, "I'm not going to lie, it is different than what I expected, but if you say we can make it work, I'm going to trust you on that. You haven't let me down yet."

I start to swoop down for a kiss, but Meshi shocks the hell out of me by grabbing a fistful of my hair and holding my head in place.

"And I never will," he growls, then pulls my face to his in a lip-crushing kiss.

His fervor only stokes my lust higher and I can feel my pounding pulse between my slick thighs. He puts a claw on my waist, pushing me into him while I dry hump him like the sex-starved maniac he's turned me into. I lose myself in the moment as his other claw palms my breast through my jumpsuit, pricking the underside with a sting that I feel directly in my clit. I'm wanton, completely unleashed, as I feel an orgasm creeping up on me. The hardness I'm grinding against seems to get impossibly thicker and the moan I release would be embarrassing if I could think coherent thoughts right now.

"That's right, my Hope. Use me. Take your pleasure from me." Meshi's voice is a ragged growl in my ear. The desperate lust in it is enough to push me over the edge into bliss.

I come with a low groan, the sound of releasing something pent up for way too long. It's not the fact that this is the first time I've been intimate with anyone in over a year, or even the fact that Meshi has worked me up for the last two weeks until I practically jumped his bones. Something else seems to break free in me, as Meshi wraps his wings around me in a warm, velvety embrace and whispers praise in my ear, and for the first time since I left Earth, I have this fantastic, bubbly feeling that everything is going to be alright.

"That was the most erotic thing I've ever experienced," Meshi proclaims when I rest my head against his chest, savoring the sound of his heart pounding in my ear.

"I can't believe I threw myself at you like that. I should be embarrassed, but... I'm not," I confess.

"Why should you be? I thoroughly enjoyed myself." He chuckles and I realize something.

"Wait, did you..?" I try to lift my head to see his face, but it's impossible with his wings around me and my arms trapped in them, as well.

"Did I imprint the memory of you coming in my mind forever? Sky, I hope so."

"No, Meshi, I mean, did you... you know?" I don't know why I'm so flustered now, but it is physically painful for me to ask, "did you come?"

"No, I did not, but that doesn't mean I enjoyed myself any less." He places a kiss on the top of my head and gives me another squeeze. "As much as I would like to unzip your worksuit and lick your pussy clean, we have a lot to do today if you want to stay on schedule for your support group."

Internally, the aforementioned pussy gives a little squeeze, letting me know where her vote goes. Externally, I groan loudly. I know he's right. Still, I take a moment to enjoy the feeling of his heartbeat against mine, letting my thoughts wander to the last two weeks.

We made a list of everything I needed to learn to be a model citizen here, and over the last two weeks we've been working through it on a schedule we made together. This is all stuff Prue would have taken care of for me in the past, telling me when to show up and what to do when I got there, and honestly, I didn't realize how much work it is.

Every day we've spent 15-20 minutes going over the datapad. Meshi quickly learned that's about all I can take before I lose my patience. Technology doesn't like me, and I'm not a big fan of it either. It's a necessary evil living on a space station like this, though, so we're covering the most important and useful things, albeit very slowly. He's also been teaching me all the different races that are represented on the station and how to greet each one. I haven't got them memorized yet, but he quizzes me daily so maybe eventually I will.

Besides all that, we've also been working on the *minklas*. We decided to make two, one for Prue and Asper, and one for Destiny and Khur, and we're having so much fun designing them and slowly crafting them together. We just finished them and plan to deliver Destiny's today.

Watching Meshi carve the crystals we picked out together two weeks ago was so captivating. He has these crazy-looking claws that are sharp enough to cut diamonds, and he's so delicate with them, so gentle and meticulous, it could break your heart. While he carved, sometimes I worked on making little discs of resin with swirls of the dye I've started making from crushed petals. Bazzel showed me how she makes her pressed flowers recently and I've been experimenting with my own version for about a week now.

In short, we've been spending a lot of time together. Meshi usually comes over around lunch time and stays past dinner. He knows all the best recipes on the nutritional printer, so I've gotten to eat food from all over the galaxy—or a proximation of it at least. He has a habit of grousing about the meals, even though I think they're mostly amazing.

Just wait until you try the real thing! He always says. I refuse to admit how cute it is.

It's strange how quickly we've fallen into our own little routine, but somehow it feels completely natural. We mostly hang out in my apartment, but today we're taking a field trip to Destiny's supply shop, where I get to learn all about how to place and pick up orders. It's also an opportunity to work on another, secret goal of mine, one that is making my stomach twist itself into knots now that I have to think about it again. I need to *sincerely* apologize to Destiny—for how I behaved at the coffee date we all had, and for how I quietly judged her.

It turns out hooking up with aliens isn't so bad, after all.

"I hate it when you're all responsible and shit," I mutter into his chest, nuzzling my cheek against his hard pecs.

"No you don't. In fact, I think that's one of your favorite things about me." He chuckles, releasing his hold on me. I plant a soft peck of a kiss to his lips before standing up and straightening my jumpsuit. I'm embarrassed again, realizing I am still completely clothed and probably look like a sex-rumpled hussy, but it dissolves when Meshi stands up and comes straight to me, wrapping me in a hug.

"Thank you, my Hope, for trusting me and being vulnerable with me." He clears his throat before continuing, "I think I've made myself clear, but let me reiterate, I am yours. From the moment I first saw you, I knew I would be yours until the day I leave this universe, and long after that. I don't want to scare you, but you—you cannot scare me off. You cannot push me away. I am waiting for you to realize that... to truly realize that, before I show you the ways that Winged-Ones, as the humans say, *make love.*"

I am, not for the first time, stunned by Meshi's words. I want to protest, to tell him it's only physical, a chemical reaction or something in our hormones, but I can't bring myself to speak the words. It feels wrong to downplay what we have, and while I am absolutely not ready to acknowledge or admit to what this is, I don't think I can verbally refute it either.

18

Meshi

I'm so proud of Hope. Over the last few weeks, I've watched her bloom into one of Sanctuary's most beautiful flowers. I've learned, with Hope, that oftentimes all she wants or needs is someone who will stand with her while she fixes her own problems. She's smart, capable, driven, she doesn't want anyone to save her. Just someone to be there for her while she saves herself. So that's what I will do.

I have to splash some cold water on my face in the washroom before my cock will recede back into my body, but I wasn't lying when I told Hope I don't mind if I don't orgasm. Watching her come undone on top of me was more than I could ever dream of. I knew the differences in our bodies might scare her, but my brave woman was not frightened off. In fact, I'm pretty sure by the end, she liked it.

When we leave her apartment, I make Hope navigate us to the elevators, something I've done a few times in the last two weeks. She's smart, a quick study, and by the third time, she'd navigated this division like a pro. Now her real test will be navigating *other* divisions, which are all set up similarly, but of course, with their own quirks, too.

Plus, with Hope leading the way, I have the best view in Sanctuary Station, of her round ass—the perfect clawful, as I recently discovered—and the sassy swing of her hips. I'm both utterly disappointed and unbelievably proud when we reach the elevators in a few short minutes.

"Great job, my Hope! You've got this division mapped, I'd say," I praise her, loving the way her cheeks pinken and the corners of her mouth turn up.

"Thanks, Mesh. I couldn't have done it without you."

On the elevator I gesture for her to choose the floor, letting Hope keep practicing her skills. We're alone on the elevator and she stands next to me, shoulder-to-shoulder as the lift activates with a hum. I desperately want to grab her hand, lace her fingers with my claws and feel her warm, steady heartbeat in my palm.

I refrain, though, not wanting to push my luck after such a perfect experience earlier. Almost as if she's read my thoughts, Hope slips her hand into my claw, pressing our palms together and squeezing.

"Thank you, Meshi. Sincerely, you've been amazing. I don't think I would have ever fit in here if it weren't for you."

I have all these words, fighting for attention, they create a dam in my throat, and I stutter uselessly for a moment before the elevator dings and the doors open on division 5. Hope doesn't let go of my hand as she drags me out of the elevator and in the direction of our destination. I knew she'd be able to figure it out.

The supply station is busy this morning, with a line almost out the door. Hope doesn't seem to mind, though, as she finds a spot at the back of the queue. At the front, I see Destiny is talking to an elderly Dhugaren, very obviously holding up the line. She smiles at him, nodding kindly, and any frustration washes right away. She's the perfect person for this job, patient and kind, but, according to Khur, not afraid to put the work in to get something accomplished. That's a good trait to have when you have to navigate the foreboding stacks behind the counter. The tall shelves, several times my height, go back at least 30 feet into the darkness. I am not afraid of the dark and I still shiver a bit when I see them.

On either side of the counter digital screens glow, available for citizens to put their own orders in and avoid waiting in line. I know Hope pretty well by now, though, and I know she would not want to try and figure out how to use another alien technology, even if most people would think it's fairly simple. It looks like the other citizens here today feel the same as Hope, preferring to wait in line rather than use the self-service screen.

"Hellooo!"

A voice calls from behind us and Hope and I both turn to see the human woman that's gotten in line behind us. She's taller than Hope or her sister, though still quite a bit shorter than I am—her wild curls give her several inches in height. While Hope's deep black curls are wide, wavy and soft, framing her face and leaving her gorgeous, long neck visible, this human's curls are tightly wound, no thicker than my claw. A bright, orangeish-red color, they cascade down the length of her back like a river of fire. I have to admit, humans are a uniquely attractive species, from what I've seen so far.

No one holds a candle to my Hope, though.

"Oh gosh, Hi! It is so exciting to see another human face. I'm Merry." The woman sticks a hand out to Hope enthusiastically, giving her full attention to her.

"Hi. I'm Hope," she replies, "this is Meshi. Have you not seen any other humans since moving here?"

"Nope, but I haven't really had the best luck navigating the place. It's huge!" Merry looks around us with wide eyes, as if only now realizing the size of the station. "I heard that there's a human woman working here, though, so I wanted to come introduce myself. Is that you?"

"No, that's Destiny," I inform her, pointing towards the brunette in question, who has finally finished with the senior Dhugaren and is now helping a young Mercian mom with a fussy guppy strapped to her chest.

"Hmm.. Do you know her well? I heard through the grapevine that she's pregnant by her Dhugaren boyfriend," Merry gossips, looking back and forth between Hope and I curiously. "Looks like everyone's getting comfortable with the locals."

I try to reserve judgment, but the tone Merry uses talking about Destiny's pregnancy rubs me the wrong way. With a weird sense of deja-vu, I remember our first meeting in the meadows, when Hope seemed so disapproving of Destiny and Khur's relationship. She's changed so much in the last few weeks. I know she doesn't feel that way anymore. She was the one who insisted we come here in the first place, so she could apologize to her friend. That doesn't mean she's completely without reservation, though.

Will she pull her hand away? I won't. I am proud of this touch, this small gesture of claiming in such a public place. I will try not to be too hurt if she does, I tell myself, but instead, she surprises me by tightening her grip and shooting the woman an indignant look.

"We're all locals now, Merry. Destiny and Khur are good friends of ours and we're really happy for them." My fierce woman declares. "Do you have a problem with that?"

Merry snorts, shaking her head. "Girl, no. I'm wondering where I can get my own hunky alien."

"Well it's not like there's a shortage," Hope snorts and I shoot her an indignant look of my own. Sky above, what's that supposed to mean?

"True. I just haven't found my particular flavor yet," she muses, suddenly turning her attention to me, her eyes travelling the length of my form.

"This one is claimed," Hope snaps, stepping in front of me. "Find your own."

Her possessiveness sends electricity through my veins, making me want to open my wings to their full, impressive span. I'm surprised, but nonetheless overjoyed that she would say something like that so publicly.

Merry isn't perturbed in the least, releasing a high-pitched giggle that itches my ears. She rolls her eyes at Hope's response.

"I'm just teasing. You two are obviously together. Maybe he's got a brother or a friend he could introduce me to, though?"

My eyes go wide, thinking about Maklash, my only unmated brother, with this rather high-pitched human. It would make family gatherings even louder than they already are. Maybe she sees the uncertainty in my eyes, because Merry laughs again, swatting a hand at the air.

"I'm joking! Geez, you two are too serious."

Hope's eyes narrow, the grip on her hand becoming uncomfortably tight.

"Did you need something from the supply station or did you seriously walk all the way here to catch some gossip in real-time?" Hope snaps, the volume of her voice raising with each word. "Because that's pretty fucking gross to just come ogle someone at their job—fucking fulfillment position—whatever it's called—to fulfill your own sick curiosity."

Merry's eyes widen and the friendly grin she is wearing drops instantly.

"No! That's not what I meant to do at all!" she exclaims, putting her hands in front of her as if to ward off an attack.

I can't say I blame her, either. Hope is glaring at her hard enough to drill through rock.

"I just haven't seen any other humans here. It's been like a month since we arrived. I was getting lonely." She drops her hands, looking back out at the entrance we've shuffled away from as the line has shrunk, like she's contemplating leaving.

"Shit. No, I get that. I'm..." Hope coughs like she's choking and I give her hand a reassuring squeeze. "I'm sorry I jumped to conclusions. Let's start over. I'm Hope, and this is my boyfriend, Meshi."

She gestures to me, a mirror image of Destiny and Khur all those weeks ago, and my chest puffs with pride. I extend my free wing—the one Hope isn't holding onto for dear life—out to my side and bow in a traditional Winged-One greeting.

"Well met, Merry," I tell the baffled-looking human.

"Nice to meet you, too," she says, smiling shyly at us. "I'm glad to see some of us are fitting into this place well."

"Girl! It was not easy for me at first. Meshi's been helping a lot. I've been wanting to start some kind of human support group, though, so we can all acclimate to this place together." Hope tells her, excited now that she's gotten past her anger.

By the time we make it to the counter, Hope and Merry are chatting like old friends. The pride that fills me watching them warms my chest. Seeing Hope embracing Sanctuary Station and our way of life is a beautiful thing. Getting to be a part of that life with her, it's everything.

19

Hope

Prue and I didn't have a lot of friends after graduating high school. She skipped the third grade and I repeated the sixth, so by high school we were in the same classes, extracurriculars, everything—and when we weren't, I fixed it. I'd complain to the principal or the counselor, and if that didn't work, I got my parents involved. After a few times of that, the school learned that I was going to get my way, one way or another.

I'm not some huge spoiled brat, there's a few things I put my foot down about. One of them is Prue.

Before the end of the world, I thought we'd do everything together, always. I even found two brothers for us to date, but of course, Prue didn't like her brother. I was still looking for their replacement when the world ended. Eventually, we'd marry them, get side-by-side townhouses in Hyde Park, and plan our pregnancies so our kids were the same age.

I guess that's not going to happen now.

And maybe that's...for the best. The plans I had back then don't make sense anymore. Maybe they never did.

I can't help but glance at Meshi next to me, let my gaze devour his sharp jawline, the angular beauty of his face. If we'd followed my juvenile plan, I'd never have met him. That's what it seems now, looking back at how I thought our life would look. So juvenile and silly. If we'd been with those brothers, we may not have survived long enough to get rescued by the Originem. Prue would never have met Asper, and as terrified as I am for her, I am also secretly, very excited to be an aunt. I would have loved to do the whole mom thing with her, but you never know. Maybe next time...

"Earth to Hope—Oh! Ain't that funny, we can't say that anymore, can we?"

Merry's southern twang pulls me out of my daydream and I look up to see we're right in front of the service desk, with Destiny's effervescent smile beaming from the other side.

"Hey Hope. Hi Meshi, it's so good to see you two. I was hoping you'd come visit."

Her smile is so sweet and guileless, I immediately feel more at ease. Behind her the rows and rows of supplies for all the different species on the station really do look creepy as fuck, exactly like Destiny told me, but she seems to be getting along fine. Next to her, there's a huge pile of packages in all sorts of sizes. I guess the supply station also functions as an outgoing postal service?

"Hey girl, I brought something for you, but let me introduce you to my new friend, first. I have a feeling you guys are gonna hit it off," I speculate, waving at Merry to step up to the counter where Meshi and I are leaning on our elbows. Well, I'm leaning on my elbows. Meshi is standing behind me with his wings on my waist and his chin kind of resting on top of my head. I'm trying desperately not to notice how warm and cozy, how safe and shielded and loved it makes me feel because I might spontaneously combust. In one day we went from the equivalent of project partners who sometimes kiss to...committed? Is that what we are now?

"The name's Merry!" she says when I take too long to speak, thrusting her hand out towards Destiny.

She takes it, and it's a little comical with their height difference and the long counter in the way.

"Merry hasn't seen any other humans since she arrived," I tell Destiny pointedly. She'll get the hint.

"Oh, honey, do you live on this division? You're coming over for dinner tonight. I'm the only human in a herd of Dhugarens, but you get used to the growling." As expected, Destiny immediately starts taking Merry under her wing and I mentally revise my plans for a support group. A mentor program would work well, too. Maybe both. A human support group and experienced citizen mentor program might be helpful. Meshi has been invaluable to my orientation.

"Girl, I'm from Texas. A little bit of growling ain't gonna scare me." Merry giggles, and I swear I feel Meshi cringe behind me. "Besides, you're the talk of the town and I gotta know more about this bun you're baking."

I legitimately can't control how my eyes roll at her theatrics.

"Apparently, everyone knows about your condition," I tell Destiny quietly. I still can't help but be a little worried about her and my sister. What if the Originem decide they don't want intermingling like that?

"Yeah, well, Furga can't keep a secret for shit." Destiny rolls her eyes back at me, but there's no heat in her voice. "I know she's just excited, so I can't really be mad. Plus, I won't lie and say I don't love the attention."

Meshi has told me a bit about his brother, Shemo, and Destiny's Dhugaren friend, Furga. Apparently they've been in love for ages, but they were afraid to be the first interplanetary couple on the station. As soon as Destiny and Khur announced their engagement and pregnancy, Shemo popped the question. Though, according to Furga, they're going to have an extended engagement.

"Attention?" Meshi asks Destiny.

She gestures to the pile of packages next to her and then to the line behind us, still trailing out the door. The sweet smile that lights up her face makes my heart swell to three times its size.

"All these people are coming to see me. Some just introduce themselves and congratulate me. Some people bring gifts and advice. It's—" She chokes up a bit and I'm going to blame her pregnancy hormones. "—It's honestly been one of the sweetest things."

She barely keeps herself together and I know what I'm about to say is going to dredge up the waterworks for real. It's gotta be done, though.

"Actually, Meshi and I brought you a gift, too." I elbow Meshi, unnecessarily, because he's already pulling our carefully wrapped gift out of his workbag. It's wrapped in some fabric from one of Meshi's old jumpsuits, and tied with a bow I dyed myself, and I can't help but to puff my chest out as Destiny carefully unwraps it and holds it to the light.

The baby mobile is made from three concentric circles. Around the outermost circle, we tied the resin discs, filled with colorful flowers, in different heights. We did the same with brightly colored crystal shards, no bigger than my pinkie. The piece de resistance, though, what made this baby mobile, and all Winged-One *minklas*, I'd recently learned, special, was what hung in the very center.

Carved into a five-sided tower with a point at the bottom, a guardian quartz, only found Bejkarr, and now the Caverns, glowed of its own accord. It shines its soft white light through the colorful crystals and the flower petals around it and casts kaleidoscopes across the walls for the kit to watch.

I explain this all to Destiny as she inspects it, holding it up this way and that, letting the light catch the different charms we've hung around it. Then I take a deep breath, gearing up to say those two little words, but before I can speak, she starts crying in earnest.

I vault over the countertop in a flash, almost knocking Meshi's chin in the process. He barely steps back in time and Merry follows me over seconds later. I gently take the mobile and lay it on the counter while Merry pulls a tissue out of nowhere and offers it to her. When the two of us wrap Destiny in a big group hug, Meshi tells everyone still waiting in line that the depot is closed for the day and to please come back tomorrow. I don't think I'll ever get used to the way his "take-charge" voice, as I've started calling it, sends shivers down my spine. There's something so self-assured, so confident and competent about it, that makes me want to hand over all control to him, and him alone.

"Aww, guys, I'm fine now, really." Destiny says after we've hugged for a few minutes and the crowd in the depot is cleared out. She wipes her cheeks a few times and sighs before turning to me with a watery grin. "At least I'm not the only one acting crazy. Prue has been a hormonal mess the last few days."

A pang hits my chest at that knowledge. I should be there for her. I *want* to be there for her. A loud gasp makes me turn to Merry's wide-eyed face, though.

"Oh my god! Are you saying there's another woman pregnant? Already? My goodness, these aliens must be fertile little turtles."

Destiny snorts, "Nothing little about it honey, and my friend has not gone public yet, so please keep that to yourself."

I barely notice Merry mime zipping her mouth closed because my vision is starting to tunnel a little. What she said, about the aliens being super fertile, makes me realize that in all of the anticipation of getting physical with Meshi, I kind of forgot that sex might create babies. I mean, I assumed that we couldn't procreate, but obviously that's not right. Hell, Merry may very well have a point. The two people I know who fucked aliens are now pregnant. That's a 100% success rate. Holy shit, I may pass out.

"Hope, you okay, babe?" Merry's cheery voice barges into my mental spiral and I have the capacity to nod and force a smile at her and Destiny. I take a few deep breaths before speaking and my mind feels a bit clearer.

"Yes. If you don't mind, Meshi and I are going to head out. Destiny, I just really wanted to say how happy I am for you and how I can't wait to meet the little cutie." I give her a quick hug, then Merry, too, so she doesn't feel left out. I've never been a hugger, but I guess it's not so bad when we're leaving, or someone is especially hormonal.

Right now, my mind is all over the place. I've been hit with so many revelations in the last few hours and I need to process everything. Meshi helps me back over the counter, even though, as Destiny points out, there is a partition we could lift and walk through. I like to feel his claws on my thighs as he hoists me up there, though. I lace our fingers together as we exit the depot.

"What troubles you, my Hope?" Meshi asks, his words and tone commanding me to lay my troubles out for him.

So I do.

"Do you think... the Originem have ulterior motives? For Sanctuary Station, for all of us? I mean, they aren't making any money here. In fact, I'm sure it costs them a lot to keep this place running." It's something that's been eating at me for a while.

"Well, before I answer your question, I would like to point out that's a very capitalistic view of our situation, and the Originem are vocally opposed to capitalist ideology," he informs me as we leave the supply station.

Around us, the market is bustling with citizens of all kinds. I want to ogle at everything, but this conversation needs to happen first.

"Well, yeah. It's hard to wrap my mind around that," I admit.

"I think you get used to it. It's all I've ever known. Regardless, though, to answer your question, yes. I do believe they have ulterior motives that we are not aware of. That doesn't necessarily mean they're malevolent motives, though. I think anyone who believes the Originem has been completely forthcoming with us are naive fools. But I have a good life here. A home and a family I may not have otherwise."

He pauses as we pass a group of bright orange aliens with tentacles haggling with a tall, dark grey Dhugaren.

"I understand how hard it must be for you to trust again," he continues once we can hear each other again, "but don't rob yourself of a good thing, a good life, because you fear having it stolen."

He's right. He's so right it hurts a little. I've been so scared for so long, letting that fear drive me to push everyone away, rather than let them get close enough to hurt me. I'm tired of feeling scared all the time. With Meshi's hand in mine, I know I don't have to be scared anymore.

Nodding, I pull him into the market. Time to start living. Right now.

20

Hope

We explore the market on Division 5 for a while and I'm impressed and awed over and over again at the skillful, creative work I see. Some booths have huge woven tapestries in all sorts of colors and textures, with intricate scenes depicted in the weaving. Others display pottery similar to the mugs Meshi and Destiny shattered during that disastrous coffee date. Still other booths have different kinds of alien street food, tech, and any other number of things I can't actually recognize. Meshi fills me in when I ask, but otherwise he seems content to follow along and listen to me geeking out about all the sights surrounding us.

Eventually the booths thin out and we're in a tall, empty, chrome corridor that could have been on any division on the station. High above us, the Winged-One's doors shine like beacons.

Following my gaze, Meshi asks me quietly, uncertainly, "Would you like to meet my mother?"

His dark eyes find mine and I realize that I do. I really do want to meet his mom and ask her what Meshi was like as a child. I want to ask her to teach me to cook his favorite meal and to tell me about

Winged-One dating culture so I can surprise him. I want to know what his fears are and what he thinks the future looks like.

Shit.

I think I might be falling in love with him. My first instinct is to fight it. Deny it. Shove it aside because that is a surefire way to get myself hurt worse than ever before.

He's asking me to meet his mom, though. Over the last two weeks, Meshi has been the most caring, kind, patient male I've ever met. He's not going to hurt me. Seeing the vulnerability in his eyes, I realize, I can't hurt him, either.

So I nod. "Yes, Meshi. I really do."

Their apartment isn't far. It's a ten minute walk and a much quicker than normal elevator lift. Soon, we're in front of an unassuming door and I'm sweating bullets. I'm anxious about a lot of things. Do the Originem have good intentions? Are we safe here? What happens if an asteroid hits the station? However, I am not the kind of person who is normally nervous about meeting people or speaking to strangers. Usually, I couldn't give a fuck what anyone thinks of me.

So the nervousness that's crept up on me during the walk over here is new and I hate it. It sits somewhere between my chest and throat like a beehive, and I'm afraid if I open my mouth the bees will come pouring out and I'll say something stupid to his mom. Most people say stupid, thoughtless things and they look like idiots for a second.

When I do it, it inevitably always hurts someone I care about. It's the worst defense mechanism ever.

"Hey." Meshi's voice pulls me out of my spiral, like it always does. "She's going to love you. Honestly, she's been asking to meet you for weeks now."

He ducks his head like he's bashful, but that makes me feel weirdly warm and melty, realizing that Meshi's been pining for me for weeks now, enough that his mom knows about me. That's some pretty serious pining. Knowing how he feels, never having to guess whether he feels the same as I do, is freeing. It gives me the permission to just...*feel it.* I really want his mom to like me, but if she doesn't that's ok. Because he definitely does. He's made it clear from day one he'd be my ride or die. Maybe this is a test, but I don't think so. Meshi is sincere, *earnest*, right down to his bones.

With that comforting knowledge and his dark eyes peering down at me in reassurance, I step up to the door. He doesn't miss a beat, swiping the reader with his wristlet, and together we walk into his home.

The apartments may be similar in layout and design, but the contrast between this one and my own is glaringly obvious. From the comfy-looking throw pillows on the recessed sectional to the many photos adorning the walls, this place is full of love and shared life. This place is a *home,* and the Winged-One female coming out of the kitchen with her wings spread wide in welcome is obviously Meshi's mom.

Her slender frame is draped in a dress, or possibly several layers of sheer scarves that flutter around her wings as she walks. Her head is hairless, like all Winged-One's I've seen, but she's painted a mandala on her crown in a bright orange that pops against her deep brown skin. Her eyes are dark, like Meshi's, and warm as she takes me in.

"Ma, I want to introduce you to my friend, Hope." His word choice almost stings, but then I realize he's probably saying that for my benefit—letting me choose how much to share, or not share about our relationship, with his mom. The problem is, I don't quite know the answer to that, either, at the moment.

She's slightly shorter than Meshi, but still plenty taller than me, so when she wraps me in a hug, her height combined with the layers of swishy fabrics, make me feel cocooned in a warm cloud. She hugs me for several seconds, squeezing tight, and I sink into her completely against my will. Any nervousness I had is completely washed away with her embrace.

"It's so nice to finally meet you, Hope. You may call me Shamara," she says, still gripping my elbows in her claws. "Why don't we go to the kitchen and have some *subus* and get to know each other? Meshi introduced me to the drink recently and I admit, I am smitten."

I'm ushered into the kitchen between Shamara and Meshi, then placed into a seat at the table. They both go to the nutrition printer and watching Meshi fuss over his mother makes a warm, rosy feeling rise in me. Soon enough, she relinquishes to him and comes to sit next to me while he fixes our drinks. I tear my gaze away from the purely masculine spread of his shoulders and find her staring at me knowingly.

"So, Hope, tell me about yourself. Meshi told me you haven't been on Sanctuary Station for long?"

"Oh, um, It's been about a month now. I feel like I'm just starting to settle in," I stutter. "All thanks to Meshi, honestly."

"Mmh. That's my boy. He's always been like that—always ready to jump up and help a friend in need." Her words are pleasant, but her tone is one hundred percent meddling mama. The way her eyes cut to Meshi's back at the word *friend* deserves an award, honestly.

When his head whips around and meets her eyes with an exasperated huff, I can't keep back the giggle I've been holding any longer. It's carefree when it leaves my lips and when both Winged-Ones turn their gazes onto me my cheeks hurt from the smile I'm fighting.

"You two are cute together. Kind of reminds me of my family, back on Earth. We were always teasing and poking each other. Prue and I still do, or did, I suppose." My smile drops as I realize this is getting kind of depressing and I divert my attention to the first thing that catches my eye—a gorgeous, intricately carved geode in the middle of the table.

Picking it up with care, I bring the little statue towards me to inspect closer. Staring into its depth is like getting lost in an MC Escher painting made of pastels and stained glass. Staircases no taller than my pinky finger change directions impossibly, while cleverly placed windows peek through to the other side of the carving, revealing repeating patterns and shapes carved with such fine attention to details I have to hold my breath as I bring my nose closer to squint at them. A soft gasp next to me shifts my focus once more. Eyes shining with unshed tears, Meshi's mother looks at me with such emotion I place the statue gently back onto the table and reach out to grab her hand.

"I'm sorry, I shouldn't have grabbed it like that," I apologize immediately, the words coming easy, thoughtlessly, as I try to take the grief out of this sweet woman's eyes.

"Oh, no. I'm sorry. It's not that, really. I'm glad you looked at it like that—really appreciated it. You should do that, whenever you want," she expresses. "Meshi's father made that for me, for our betrothal. It's our *infinium*—a tradition on Bejkarr where the males carve a geode as a gift when they propose. It's supposed to be a symbol of what they promise to fill their lives with. Common carvings are warm hearths, these stylized things of mothers holding babies. He knew I'd hate anything like that though."

Her sigh is long and filled with a melancholy that threatens to reach in and crack my hard shell. She picks up the geode between us and turns it in her fingers as Meshi deposits two steaming mugs in front of each of us and fetches his own off the sleek chrome countertops before settling into the chair across the table. Neither of us speak as Shamara gathers her thoughts.

"When he gave this to me, he said it was a promise to follow me wherever I might want to go." Her claw gently traces a hidden staircase or pathway in the carving. "Even if neither of us sees where it leads in the end."

Meshi told me about his Dad during our many conversations over my own kitchen table as we worked on our projects together. He told me about how he was killed before they'd been granted visas to move to Sanctuary Station. He was still a baby and doesn't have any memories of him. Though our losses weren't exactly the same, it made me relate to him in a way I hadn't understood before. We'd both lost parents and planets, two vital parts of our identities stripped away. I felt unbearably sad and guilty when I realized that one of the few things we had in common, possibly everyone here had in common, was loss.

Since then, I've found we have a lot more in common than that. We both love music, and he's been introducing me to different styles from different races around the station, but one of our favorites is actually his brother's band. I don't think he'd ever admit how much we play their streams on his data pad while we tinker. We also both *love* to tinker. Mine is usually the more creative, lawless side of things—pushing flower dye around liquid resin in fractions of inches until I'm satisfied with the results, while his is more practical and technical—he loves wrapping the long crystal wands we find in wire for the mobiles. The perfectly pressed lines, the intricate geometry he creates in the enclosures, are works of art, but much more organized and disciplined than my chaotic pieces. Together on the *minklas*, the juxtaposed components compliment each other well.

Looking at the depth of emotion pouring off of Shamara, I bet her and Meshi's father had the same chemistry, or something just as catalytic as ours. I stay quiet, not quite knowing how to express how I feel, but I squeeze her hand in solidarity. It's Meshi that breaks the silence."And he hasn't broken his promise, Mama. I feel him watching over me all the time."

She smiles and cups his cheek in a gentle claw. I take a deep sip of my steaming mug of *subus* to mask the emotion clogging my throat. Meshi's been playing around with the recipe a bit and he's recently found this creamer-like liquid in the nutritional printer's menu that makes it taste so close to the hazelnut lattes I used to get at home that I hum a little every time I take that first sip. I refrain this time, barely.

"I do, too, my son." She rises gracefully, all flowing fabrics and graceful limbs, and leans in to place a surprising kiss to my forehead.

"Welcome to the family, Hope. I look forward to getting to know you more another day. For now, I think I'm going to take a nap."

She glides out of the kitchen like a ballerina instructor, wings tucked into one of the many layers of her sleeves, a perfect mix of haughty and humble. I take a sip from my mug and turn towards Meshi, a witty joke on the tip of my tongue about his mama boy tendencies. Not that I would actually mean it...The whole mama boy thing really works for him. Perhaps because it is so genuine.

His expression stops me, though. Before he opens his mouth, I know what he's going to say. In that breath before he speaks, I see every moment of our life after that, like a lightning bolt has come down precisely in this moment and struck me right in the chest. "I have something for you," he croons, his eyes confident and hopeful.

"Wait!" I shout.

That lightning bolt, like when I get an idea for a new painting or mural, spurs me into action. I jump to my feet and turn towards the door.

21

Meshi

No sooner has she turned towards the door than she's turning back to me, capturing my jaw in her soft hands and leaning over me in my chair.

"I'm not running away from you, I promise." She says, placing soft kisses on my lips between words.

I nod, giving her a reassuring smile between kisses. I know she won't run now. I have been paying attention to my Hope and I have watched throughout the day as all the remaining barriers between us, everything she had been using to hold herself back, fell away. I have been waiting for this day to come, and now that it has, if Hope needs a few hours to prepare herself, I can certainly be patient a little while longer.

"I just...I have to do something first," she mutters, kissing the tip of my nose and the ridges on my brow. "Do you trust me?"

"Always, my Hope." It's the truth, even if I am extremely confused right now.

"Then bring whatever it is you have for me to my apartment for dinner tonight," she commands me. "Give me at least...five hours, okay?"

I nod again and chase her lips with my own until she gives me one last goodbye kiss. Then she turns and all but runs back out of the kitchen. I hear the swish of the front door opening and closing and I sit there for several more minutes before I take our mugs to the cleaner below the printer.

Hope arrives at her own front door about a minute after I do. She almost runs into me in her mad sprint down the corridor. Swiping her wrist over the reader, she pulls me into her apartment without saying a word.

"First of all, I want to say I'm sorry," Hope pants once we're inside. "I know I ran out on you earlier when you were about to give me, like, a really serious, meaningful gift."

She stops, panting a bit more and smiling sheepishly with a wave at her hand when I reach out to her, concerned.

"I'm fine, just out of breath. I had to grab one more thing." She shows me the wrapped bundle tucked under her arm.

Her breaths start to even as she continues on, "but I should warn you that is kind of common with me. Sometimes when I get an idea in my head, I can't help but jump straight in—feet first! I've been trying to work on myself, but...I don't think that's ever going to change."

"I don't want you to change, my Hope," I assure her, a bit flummoxed as to where she's going with this.

"Good, because I want you to give me what you wanted to give me earlier. I'm ready now."

My mother couldn't have had better timing than if we'd planned it together when she told Hope about her and my father's *infinium*. Sometimes I really do think she might have a touch of telepathy, though she'll never admit it. The point, though, is that I wouldn't be surprised if Hope knew what I meant when I told her I had a gift for her. She's a clever girl, and I was not subtle.

I am simply ready to love her, without restraint.

I pull the *infinium* I've lovingly carved in secret over the last few weeks out of my workbag. Still wrapped in cloth for protection, I slide the heavy piece across the table towards her. Without a word, Hope reaches under her arm and grabs her own wrapped bundle. She pushes it across the table until it's directly in front of my shocked face.

"Do you have a speech prepared, or should I open it?" She asks me, a tease in her voice.

I have to clear my throat twice before answering.

"I had...words...but it seems they've left the station," I stutter out, hands tracing the shape beneath the cloth lovingly.

"Well, I have words. Then we can open them together," she informs me confidently.

"I've never been in love before," she starts. "I thought I had, on Earth, with silly boys I was infatuated with, but today, I learned that is not the case. The realization hit me like a lightening bolt. I love you. I love how caring and attentive you are, how supportive, how kind and funny. You make me a better person, and when I realized, after your mom explained *infiniums*, that you were going to give me one, I knew I couldn't let you do that unless I had something to give back to you. You've given me so much in the past few weeks already. It's important to me that you know this is a partnership."

Her dark brown eyes meet mine across the table and the small smile she graces me with is full of longing and anticipation, but most of all, she looks at me like I am the most important thing in the world.

"Hope, my sweet Hope. I have loved you since the moment I first saw you, painting a protest mural in a dark hallway with bug spray and industrial cleaner. I have just been waiting for you to catch up."

"Wait...since the mural? We didn't meet until like a week after I painted that."

"It was four days. Four excruciating days during which I scoured the station for any information about you. I was desperate to know you," I confess.

"That's...actually really sweet. I thought I was so alone that day..." Her eyes get a faraway look in them briefly before she returns to the present and smiles at me. "Together, then?"

"Together."

I carefully peel the cloth away from the object in front of me. It's light and precarious feeling, like it might tip over if I'm not gentle. Next to me, Hope gasps and I chuckle because I know she ripped the wrapping off much quicker than me. I don't mind though. I appreciate that we have such different approaches to everything. Nothing like a little sweet anticipation.

Finally, my gift is revealed to me and I can't help but gasp as well. Hope used wire to create a standing mobile with a round base. Three thin, metal rods rise from the bottom, one directly in the middle with a *nifrin* about 8 inches from the base. On either side, Hope used wire to make two crude figures, a winged one and a tiny, 3-inch tall human flying a Silfan Wind Rider, flying around the *nifrin.* The wind rider has a trail of tiny crystal shards weaving in wire behind it, emulating their flower trains perfectly.

The sculpture is beautiful, but that doesn't surprise me. I've seen Hope's artistic skills in action several times over the last few weeks and I know I'm not biased when I say that she is one of, if not THE most talented artists in this entire space station.

What does surprise me is the subject it captures, because the *infinium* I gave to Hope depicts the exact same thing. Rising from the jagged, but stable bottom I left raw and uncut, two figures twirl around each other in flight. A winged-one and a human with short, wild hair riding a wind rider, whose flower train creates a colorful, swirling cyclone. I carved it directly from a geode that had plenty of vibrant fluorite inclusions. White, green and purple hues wink merrily at Hope as she twists and turns her gift, inspecting it from all angles.

"It's perfect, Meshi. So does this mean our life will be full of flying? Is that how these *infinium* work?"

"I started making this after we went flying together, that one time you put me in my place in the meadows?" I quirk a self-deprecating smile towards her so she knows there's no hard feelings. "I knew then I was never going to win you over with words. You needed deeds. Actions. I suppose I chose to carve us flying together because I wanted to make you smile like you did in the sky that day, every day, for the rest of our lives."

"Meshi..." Hope whispers, sending shivers down my wings.

"I know we haven't known each other long, but I want to be joined with you by both Winged-One and human customs. I want you to be my wife and my mate." I studied up on human commitment ceremonies and found I really like the idea of their wedding ceremonies. Hope would look beautiful in white, with her wild, black curls and her creamy pale skin.

She may not understand it, but being close with her, building the *minklas* together, and making her *infinium* in secret, has made me feel more like a Winged-One than I have in my entire life.

"I'm happy to do whatever ceremonies you want to," she tells me. "I don't really care about that kind of thing, honestly, but I do love a good party."

She hesitates, running her fingertips over the wings on the flyer in her sculpture.

"There is one thing we should discuss," she mumbles, clearing her throat several times. "I don't know if you caught what Merry said about humans being very...fertile with other...citizens, but we need to be on the same page before we have any happy little accidents."

She chuckles, finally allowing her eyes to rise and meet mine. Reaching over, I capture her restless hand and hold it in my claw.

"Hope, do you speak of children?"

"Yep," she says, popping her lips at the end. It's something she does when she's nervous and I almost laugh. Confessing love? She's confident as ever. Talking about babies though? For some reason, this woman is turning into a bundle of nerves.

"Hope, I will be happy with however many kits you choose to bless us with," I tell her, admittedly, a little confused.

"Well that's fine and all, but how many do *you* want? And when? Because I don't think there's any birth control on this station and from what I gather, odds are if we fuck, we're making a baby."

It takes everything in me to remain seated when she mentions us *fucking*, as the humans like to call it. There is a primal, archaic need to swing Hope over my shoulder and carry her all the way to the Caverns, to the private room you can reserve for special occasions that has been on my mind since this morning when Hope gyrated against my length until she blessed me with the most beautiful sounds I've ever heard come from another being.

"I admit, I would enjoy a big family, but I am not the one who carries the child. Perhaps it is a cultural difference, but Winged-One males do not choose their family size, so I don't know how to answer you fully, except to say, however many children you bless me with, I will love, cherish, and protect with all that I am."

Hope stares at me for a long moment, looking almost as confused as I feel.

"On Earth, it was usually a joint decision," she explains. "Most people try to stay within their means, only have as much family as they can afford, that kind of thing. A lot of those barriers are nonexistent here. The apartments would get crowded eventually, though."

I snort a laugh.

"They have larger apartments you can request," I murmur, my tone becoming something more serious than I intended. "When we moved here, we'd just lost our dad. I think Ma chose the smaller apartment so we'd *have* to share rooms. No one would ever be alone."

"Like me and Prue. We've always had each other." Sadness flits across her face for a second, but I see it. "I want that for my kids—our kids—one day, too. I want at least two. Maybe more. I don't know."

Her lips quirk up and she rises to her feet, abandoning the sculpture she'd been fidgeting with. She walks over to my seat with gliding, graceful steps and hooks an arm around my neck, leaning in to press her lips to mine.

"I think we should just let fate decide," she whispers against my mouth when our kiss breaks. "I'm ready for you to show me the ropes now."

22

Hope

"Do you trust me?" Meshi asks.

"I mean, I kinda thought it was obvious at this point," I tease him, but at his stern look I amend my answer. "Of course I do."

We're back on division sixteen, in the Caverns. As soon as I told Meshi what I wanted he led me straight here, into a small, private cave-like room with a locking door. The rough stone walls are lit with the soft glow of strategically placed *nifrin* crystals around the smooth, stone floor. It's pleasantly warm in here, none of the chilled draftiness one would expect in a cave on Earth.

"Thank you, Hope. I'll never stop cherishing that gift. From this point on, I need you to do everything I tell you. Can you do that?"

"Yes," I reply instantly. I'm not usually one for taking orders, especially in the bedroom, but for Meshi, I'd give about anything a try. In fact, as soon as my agreement leaves my lips, I realize I'm eager to follow Meshi's orders. Anything he might ever command of me will be for my own benefit, my own pleasure. I truly do trust him. My heart beats against my ribcage at the thought. I hope I never get used to this feeling.

"Give me a word," he says as he leans down to get something out of his trusty workbag. That thing has everything, as he proves when he pulls out a long, coiled length of black rope. "A word that when you say it will tell me to stop whatever we're doing immediately."

"Like a safe word?" I ponder it for a moment. "How about flower?"

"Flower. Got it," he agrees.

He's standing in front of me again, uncoiling that rope with sharp, deft claws. I want to reach out to him, put my arms around him, but I refrain, getting the sense that he wants to run the show here. It's such a change from everyday Meshi in some ways, but the confident, earnest aura he exudes is one-hundred percent the male I know.

"We don't have to do it this way every time we're intimate, but it's best we do it the first few times," he tells me calmly. "I would never want to hurt you."

There's no bed, no couch, only an empty, round-ish cave with rough walls, a smooth floor, and...a silver hook glinting from the ceiling. My gulp is audible in the quiet room.

"What's that for?" I point at the ceiling, my voice sounding tinny.

"You're not getting nervous now, are you, my fierce Hope?" His tone, teasing and self-assured, makes my nipples tighten noticeably.

I shake my head, but keep my feet still, despite my body leaning towards him as if I'm being pulled into his gravity. He flies up to the ring above our heads with one downward thrust of his wings, looping the rope around it and securing it with steady hands. When he's back in front of me, one end of the rope still clutched in his claws, a shiver rocks through me. Meshi, the least monstrous male I know, plays one very well, with his lithe, winged figure in the dimly lit hidden cave, holding a rope tied to the ceiling. The entire scene is so erotic my panties are undoubtedly soaked despite the fact that he has not even touched me yet.

"Take your jumpsuit off. Let me see your beauty," he commands and I jump to obey.

I've got my shoes kicked to the side and my jumpsuit around my waist before I realize he probably wanted me to take them off sexily—put on a show for him. For a moment, I worry about looking too eager, about not looking "sexy enough," but Meshi's deep, hungry growl stops my train of thought in its tracks. I look up to see his devouring gaze.

"Did you just growl?" I ask, incredulous.

Who is this male who barks commands and growls at my uncovered body? I kind of like him.

"You look good enough to eat," he groans. "Come here. I want to look at you."

There's a mere three feet between us, but my legs carry me forward before my brain registers the command, until I can feel the heat of his body in front of me. His dark eyes don't leave my face for several, agonizing seconds, and when he does look further down at my nakedness, I feel his gaze like fire across my skin. My nipples pebble almost painfully, exposed to the air and his intent stare.

"What are these?" He asks, teasing the waistband of my underwear.

Without waiting for an answer, his claw slips under the fabric and slices it clean through, leaving one leg of my panties hanging on awkwardly. The rope brushes my shoulder as he drops it and slices the other claw through the opposite leg of my panties. All I have to do is widen my stance a bit and the useless fabric flutters to the ground.

An incomprehensible noise escapes me as I stand in front of Meshi, completely nude.

He growls again, the sounds deep and sonorous, and drops to his knees in front of me. His claws wrap around to clutch my ass cheeks and my own hands fly to his head—and those sensitive ears, the best handlebars—when he leans forward and licks my slit with that inhumanly long tongue of his.

My moan fills the cavern as a wave of pleasure starts at my clit and spreads throughout my entire body. His claws prick my sensitive skin, pulling me closer and tilting his chin up to change his angle. I'm forced to widen my stance and hold on for dear life as Meshi nuzzles himself further into the apex of my thighs.

The intrusion is immediate and all-encompassing, the entirety of my attention centering between my legs. His tongue is longer than any human's and it slides between my lips, exploring my folds, making my legs shake and tremble. When he starts focusing on my clit, lapping at it with steady pressure, my orgasm barrels towards me faster than I've ever experienced before. It shocks me with its intensity and Meshi's upper body strength alone keeps me from collapsing onto the floor.

He slows his pace, pulling back some of his initial enthusiasm, delicately mapping every inch of my pussy. My oversensitive clit throbs and I cry out as he passes it and laps at my dripping entrance. The grunting, growling sounds he makes when he tastes my release sends an aftershock of pleasure through me that leaves me tingling. Just when I think I might truly collapse, or maybe die—can one die from pleasure? A timeless debate—he pulls away, keeping me steady with his claws at my waist.

“You taste how I imagine clouds would taste,” he moans. His mouth and chin are shiny in the dim light.

“Kiss me, Meshi,” I plead, cupping his jaw and pulling him up towards me.

As his mouth finds mine, my hands scramble at the tab of his zipper, desperate to feel his bare skin against mine. I never thought the metallic sussurus of a zipper would be so erotic. That random thought pops in my head as my hands burrow into his jumpsuit, relishing the satiny soft feel of his hard muscles. Any thoughts or rules or commands are lost momentarily as we devour each other. Our mouths fight for dominance briefly before he wins, invading my mouth with that wicked tongue. When my hands slip below his waistband, he growls and pulls away with a growl.

“As much as I am enjoying this, we should consider the ropes before we go much further,” he informs me begrudgingly.

"Wh—what are they for again?" I ask in a breathless whisper.

“How about I show you?" He grabs the rope dangling by our side and slides a measured length between his two claws. “Turn around, my Hope."

I do, without hesitation.

“I'm going to tie your arms and tether you to that ring up there," he tells me as he grabs one wrist, then the other, gently positioning them on either side of the back of my neck, with my elbows pointing up and out. “The purpose of this is to limit your movements, so that I can control the depth of my movements. It's an exercise in complete trust."

I stay silent as he loops the fibers around my shoulder and armpit and then around my chest, not wanting to distract him from his work.

As he knots, he talks, explaining why this became important to his people.

"As I mentioned before, we evolved to copulate in flight. Our cocks are much longer than normal to compensate for that. When we were forced into caves, our cocks didn't shrink the way that our skies did. We had to learn new ways to love each other," he explains, his hands gentle across my skin as he tightens the rope.

Something about this moment feels so profound. The intimacy of his gentle, precise claws across my bare skin as he tells me about how his people learned to love each other is somehow more powerful, feels more vulnerable, than when he had his face buried in my pussy. My heart, my very soul, fills with a light buoyant feeling.

"Is it always the female who is bound?" I whisper.

Meshi's movements stumble, ever so slightly, and I wonder if I've messed up this scene he's built, broken one of the rules. He never told me not to speak, though. I know him better than that. When he buries his face in my neck, next to where my fist is tied, and licks my exposed nape I shudder. There's nothing I could do that Meshi would think is wrong.

Now, or ever.

"It is...traditional for the female to be bound, but my Hope, you can tie me up any day, in any way."

His teeth scrape the tender skin of my neck before he withdraws, pulling on another dangling loop of rope I hadn't seen before in the low light and lifting me ever so slightly. I rise onto the balls of my feet, my heels an inch or so off the ground. I could possibly rock or swing my body if I tried, like a giant pendulum, but besides that I'm completely immoble.

I hadn't considered this specific factor when he started tying me up. I'd heard about shibari, or at least seen some incredibly sexy pictures of women tied up hanging from elaborate webs of ropes, but I hadn't considered *myself* in one of those poses. One part of my brain is thrilled to be at Meshi's mercy. Knowing he can do whatever he wants to my very willing body makes my pussy clench all over again.

The anxious part of my brain does not like that I can't move. What if there's an emergency? What if Meshi leaves? He would never leave me here...but what if he did?

My breaths start to shorten, coming in little bursts as my eyes dart around the empty stone room.

"Hush, hush, my Hope. You're okay. Just breathe."

Meshi's beautiful face steps into my line of sight and his dark eyes allow me to take a deep breath in.

"Meshi, you promise you'll untie me, right? You won't leave me like this?" Even as I ask it, I know how ridiculous I sound. My breaths are already leveling out, my panic subsiding as quick as it came.

He never brushes me off, though. Meshi takes my face in his claws, the familiar pinpricks at my jaw a welcome comfort, and ever so gently kisses my brow.

"I would never do that to you, my Hope. I will always take care of you. Would you like to continue, or would you like me to untie you? You can use your word at any time."

"No, it's okay. I want to feel you inside me."

"Good girl," he groans and I almost come right there on the spot.

His claws go to the jumpsuit that's pooled at his waist. I freeze immediately, desperate to finally see what I've already claimed as mine.

Slowly, with way more finesse than I had, Meshi drops his jumpsuit to the ground. The gasp that escapes me is completely involuntary.

When I called it a sapling earlier, I was not far off. His cock, dark brown with a thick, reddish head, is the size of a small baseball bat. It hangs almost to his knee, hard and stiff, from what I can see, but weighed down by its massive size.

"I can—I can see why we need to be careful now," I stutter. "Meshi, I'm never going to be able to take your whole cock."

I try to keep the disappointment out of my voice, but I can't help but wonder if that means we're incompatible.

"No one could. That's why we're going to learn how deep you can take me today, like this. We'll figure the rest out together...right?"

For the first time since we got here and Daddy Meshi made his appearance, he looks vulnerable. The crack in his confident facade reminds me how gentle Meshi truly is, how earnest and unguarded he is.

"Yes, baby. We'll figure it out together," I reply. "Now show me how Winged-Ones make love."

He grabs my elbows, twisting me so I have to tip toe in a circle until he's at my back again. His claws disappear and I hear him in his workbag for a moment before warm palms grasp the back of my thighs.

"I didn't bind your legs, but you should keep them pressed together. The friction will help," he informs me as he starts to rub the backs and inside of my thighs with his palms, keeping his claws carefully lifted. They're coated with some kind of oil and soon my thighs slide together without resistance. The feel of his firm massage reminds my pussy of what's to come and my wetness drips to meet the warm oil. We both groan when his wingtip touches the juncture of my thighs.

When he stands again and presses his front to my bare back, I'm panting, ready to beg him to fuck me.

I should already know Meshi is not to be rushed, though. If I've learned anything about him over the last few weeks, it's that he has unending patience. Much more than me, anyways.

"Meshi, please," I whine when he starts kissing and lapping at my nape again.

His chuckle against my ear sends goosebumps down my spine.

Finally, I feel the smooth head of his cock pushing against the back of my thighs. I squeeze them together, remembering his instructions, and painfully slowly, he pushes through my thighs and into me.

When the head of his cock finds my entrance, I realize I underestimated his size. It doesn't slide in like I expected but meets resistance that I'm desperate to push against. I stay still, though, remembering his commands.

"You're not going to hurt me, Meshi. It's okay. I want you," I pant, desperation making me ramble.

When he finally pushes into my pussy, the stretch is blissful, the pinch of pain perfection, and all I can do is moan as he withdraws slightly before pushing further in. Behind me, Meshi's growls sound almost feral, his heavy breaths puff hot on my neck. He's got a death grip on my hips, using the inertia of my hanging body to rock me into him ever so slightly, going deeper and deeper each time.

When he hits my cervix I grunt from the pressure of it all. With anyone else, I would have been immediately embarrassed, but with him, there's no room for any of that. As if he has a sixth sense, knowing every pleasure point inside of me, he applies gentle pressure there, grinding into me and bottoming out. I can tell he's still not fully sheathed, our thighs have yet to make contact, but I know I can't take another centimeter.

"Right there," he growls, pulling out and slamming in with such precision I see stars. The feel of his ginormous cock sliding through my oiled thighs adds to the myriad of sensations assaulting my being and when he slides out and slams home again, the stars I'm seeing turn to fireworks.

"I'm coming, Meshi! Holy fuck, I'm coming," I shout, trying desperately not to rock my hips into the sensation.

"Yes, my Hope, that's my good girl. Come all over this huge cock," Meshi growls into my neck, his claws reaching around to palm my breasts as his hips stutter and he unloads into me.

We stay like that for several minutes, my body inert but leaning back into his, being held by his arms around my waist, his palms cupping my breasts, and his cock deep inside of me. When he pulls out, the amount of liquid that rushes out of me is obscenely sexy and I moan a little.

He uses quick claws to slice away my bindings and when I ask about the rope he chuckles at me.

"I work in maintenance. I can get more rope," he assures me as he rubs my stiff shoulders. I lean into him, exhausted.

"That was amazing, truly, but the benefit to doing it in a bed is that we can go to sleep afterwards." I stifle a yawn. "You wore me out."

"Perhaps I'll install a hook in our bedroom. I very much like the idea of you tying me up next time."

Once we're dressed and Meshi's cleaned up the mess of rope fibers he made, he hooks his workbag low on his belt and swoops me up in his arms, bridal-style.

"I guess you're moving in with me now?" I tease. "Just inviting yourself in?"

I already figured that would happen. He's over most days anyways, and Prue's basically moved into Asper's place. I'm going to have to face them tomorrow. Tonight though, for a while longer, I don't want to think about anyone but Meshi.

"Married human couples do live together, don't they?" He's smiling, teasing me back, and my heart soars.

"I suppose they do," I reply, kissing his nose. "Now take me home."

23

Hope

Whoever said "everything looks brighter in the morning" definitely knew what they were talking about. They were probably waking up next to their soulmate, maybe even wrapped in a warm, velvety soft cocoon of wings, having little kisses sprinkled onto their bare shoulders. If I knew this was what I had to look forward to with my alien mate, I would have given in weeks ago. Any nervousness I had about what I have to do today is completely gone. In fact, I'm looking forward to seeing my sister.

We haven't spoken in weeks. I completely understand why this was necessary for her. Hell, it was necessary for me, too. I would never have stepped out of my comfort zone and into Meshi's warm, loving embrace if I had my sister around to do everything for me. Now that I've learned some independence, though, I'm ready to have her back in my life, and I really hope she feels the same.

Oh, shit. There's the nervousness.

I mean, I can't imagine that Prudence would never want to talk to me again. We've been best friends our entire lives. She's about to have my niece. I want to be a part of their lives. I know I was kind of a shitty sister, but was I so awful she'll cut me off forever?

"Hey, none of that." Meshi's soft voice filters through my panic. He tightens his embrace, blocking out the light. I snuggle deeper into his chest.

"What if she doesn't want me around anymore?" I whisper, my breath warm in the space between our bodies.

"I don't think that will be the case, my Hope. I think she's eager to have her sister back in a healthier capacity," he says gently.

I hate it when he speaks so logically.

Okay, maybe I don't, but I'm not ready to accept his rationality yet, so I press my lips to his chest and blow a loud, sloppy raspberry on his skin. In return, he reaches down and gives my ass a squeeze, the points of his claws pricking me enough to make me yelp.

"Come on. Up you go. We both need showers before we venture out today," he teases me, opening his wings and letting the cold air of the bedroom into our previously warm cocoon.

Squealing, I jump and grab his wing, pulling him with me to the bathroom across the hall.

"Come shower with me and I can show you some of the crazy things humans do with their mouths."

Meshi growls and scoops me into his wings, dashing into the bathroom on fleet feet.

Division thirteen is nothing like the others I've seen. Granted, I've only seen a few others, but Meshi says this one is unique. The entryway off the elevator has a billboard-sized screen flashing a long message in different languages. Winged-One flashes up first and he explains that this division is a fully-integrated biome. On the other side of the pressurized doors is a perfect recreation of a jungle that was destroyed by world-wide catastrophic volcanic activity. The Ferziti would not leave without it, Meshi explains, so now it's a protected nature sanctuary.

"So there are like...tigers in there?" I ask, eyeballing the doors warily.

"I don't know what a tiger is, but I know there aren't any predators. The Originem would never allow that," he consoles me, heading towards the entrance. "Come on, we have to get sanitized."

"You sure you don't blindly trust them?" I grumble, but I follow him anyway.

When we step through one set of doors, we find ourselves in a small room with another door on the far side. We stand in the circle in the middle of the room and Meshi shows me where there is a button on the floor to step on that activates blue laser lights.

"Blue-light disinfection. Protects the native plant species," Meshi explains as we're scanned and sanitized.

I messaged Prue last night before we went to bed—by myself I might add, but I'm still relieved to see my sister waiting at the entrance when the final doors open, with Asper at her side. She's already gone native, with a tube-style strapless dress in the same beige fabric as

Asper's two-piece ensemble, and bare feet. Her normally pin-straight long black hair is a bit wild, with the prettiest beachy waves in it. She's absolutely glowing, a contagious smile gracing her lips.

Turning to Asper, I tuck my hair behind one ear then clench my fist to my heart in a traditional Ferziti greeting, like Meshi taught me. In turn, she reaches out her hand and when I go to shake it, she pulls me the rest of the way into the biome and wraps me into a hug. I force my body to relax—I'm never going to be a natural hugger, and everyone is going to have to come to terms with that—and pat her on the back a few times before gently pulling myself away.

"It's so good to see you, Hope. We're so excited to have you here," Asper gushes to me, then turns to Meshi. "And you, too, Meshi. Are we all one big happy family now?"

I snort because last time Asper and Prue saw us was at that disastrous coffee date, but I mentioned that Meshi and I have been spending time together and now all of a sudden we're one big happy family? I mean, they're not *wrong*, but when did I become so predictable?

"I am optimistic that by the end of the day, we will be," Meshi replies, nudging me with his wing-joint.

"Speaking of," I hedge, taking the hint, "Prue, do you think we could talk, just the two of us, for a moment?"

"Sure, there's a clearing around the corner here." She leads me around the metal frame of the elevator bay. The only non-organic thing I can see, it sticks out like a sore thumb. Some opportunistic vines have crept up the chrome walls, but none have made much progress up the sleek surface that seems to extend up forever. The path we follow has the elevator bay on our left, but to our right is nothing but dense, verdant jungle. The kind of scene I've only ever witnessed on a television screen, my mind almost can't comprehend the vast, shadowy expanse of foliage that seems to go on forever.

The clearing she spoke of is about a football field of open space, covered in soft-looking moss, on the opposite side of the entrance. Looking at it makes me want to take my own shoes off. Past the clearing the jungle continues on forever, with no back wall in sight, like the other biomes I've visited. Surely there is one. This space station can't be infinite, after all, but the illusion of a never-ending jungle is both thrilling and terrifying.

"No tigers in here, right?" I ask Prue, just in case.

"No," she replies, laughing, "no tigers."

She settles easily onto the moss, stretching her bare legs in front of her. She looks so comfortable, so in her element here. When she pats the ground next to her, I lower myself gently to the ground.

"This place suits you."

"Thanks. I think so, too." She smiles, running her hands over the greenery around her. "I knew this place would be perfect for us, but I couldn't have imagined how it would play out."

I can't contain my snort. "Yeah, I'd say so."

She shoots me a look and I realize she won't be patient forever.

"I came to apologize to you. I'm sorry for everything. I was incorrigible when we first arrived here. Even before then, I am just now beginning to realize how much I depended on you, for everything. I shouldn't have put so much on you."

"Hope, I don't mind that you depended on me sometimes. That's what sisters are for. I just want to be able to have my own life, my own interests. I felt like I was constantly juggling *your* interests, *your* concerns. That wasn't just your fault, either." She sighs, finally looking up at me. "I'm sorry, too. I think it was often easier for me to focus on your shit than figure out my own."

"I—wow, Prue, I had no idea you felt that way."

"I know. I don't think I did, either, until I met Asper and realized I'd never really *tried* to do my own thing. I had this crazy idea, though, and she's been helping me with it. Well, really it's our idea together, but it could change everything!"

A bright, effervescent feeling rises in my chest and I lean forward, her excitement alluring and irresistible.

"We're going to open a cafe," she exclaims, gesturing at the clearing around us. "Right here in the moss. Not a building, but an open air cafe, serving *subus* and some other Ferziti cuisine, like small bites. We could put a prep counter right against the elevator shaft and I guarantee you the Originem can have a water line run from one of the other floors. We're going to need one anyways."

Prue rambles on with stars in her eyes, and I see her in a new light all over again. I had no idea that she wanted to open a coffee shop, but I have no doubt she'll make it happen. Now that I know about it, I'm going to do whatever she needs me to do to make sure it happens. With her permission of course.

"Prue, if you need *anything* from me to make this happen, please let me know! I think it's such a great idea, and not only because I love *subus,*" I tease.

"Actually, I do have an idea I think you could help with," she informs me. "Destiny said you were trying to get a human support group together, gathering contact info?"

"Mercy, gossip gets around this station fast. I didn't even tell her about that yet!"

"I know, apparently Merry was telling her about it. Earth or not, you know some girls love a good gab."

She laughs and I can't help but join her. Merry, especially, did seem to love to gab.

"Well, it's in the beginning stages, but I've got quite a few contacts in my tablet just from word of mouth. Mostly Meshi's, honestly. You want a good gab? Talk to a maintenance person on this space station. They're worse than Merry, though they'll never admit it," I confide, rolling my eyes.

It's true, though. Between Meshi, Jerrol, hell even Khur when he deigns to share with his coworkers, it seems like the maintenance people somehow end up privy to all the important gossip around here.

"Ha! Good to know. I'll be taking that advice sooner or later. For now, can you use your contacts to organize a volunteer event here? I need some hands to help me put shit together, but the Ferziti are pretty wary. Asper's the first one to ever leave," she informs me with wide eyes. "I figure a bunch of nice human women might be a good way to start introducing them to the rest of the station."

" That's a great idea. I'll start putting some messages out tonight. You should see me on the datapad. I'm a real whiz now."

"Okay, grandma. You learned how to use a tablet. Only took a few decades."

I roll my eyes. She's right, though. It was about time I caught up with everyone. I may not be a whiz with technology, not really, but at least I can function.

"Come on," I shout, jumping to my feet and reaching down to pull her up. "Meshi and I brought you guys a gift."

She keeps my hand grasped tight even after she stands up and starts walking back towards our mates. Through the trees I see them both as they turn to us and smile.

Epilogue: Meshi

Hope breezes into the kitchen, waving her instant camera in the air like a prize. Over the last six weeks, she's shown me the contraption and her scant film supply. We've been documenting some of the biomes "as the inspiration sparks." It's an interesting machine. Cameras are common enough, but instantaneous ones are unheard of here. I'm interested in the mechanics of it, but Hope won't let me take it apart until she uses all the film up.

"One left," she exclaims.

I hand her the hot cup of *subus* that I have waiting for her, brewed exactly how she likes it. The little hum she makes when she takes the first sip warms me to the tips of my ears. I get to hear that every morning. What a lucky male I am.

"Good morning to you, too," I tease her, bending down to kiss her on the nose. "I'm betting you have a great idea for this last photo, huh?"

Hope is full of great ideas. Over the last six weeks, I've become familiar with that particular sparkle in her eye. It's the plan to accompany that idea that she needs help with. I've made it my mission to help her come up with those plans.

"I want you to take it. I've been wanting an aerial shot of the Meadows forever, but I can't fly and use this at the same time," she informs me, setting the camera on the colorfully stained counter in front of me.

I could replace the chrome countertop she marred with her first ever art project here, but I don't want to. Every morning, when I come in here to make our *subus*, I'm greeted by the colorful, pockmarked metal, and it reminds me of the first time I ever saw Hope. I love this countertop, and Hope hasn't suggested replacing it, so I won't.

"I can do this for you."

Careful of the mug she's clutching, I pull her towards me, wrapping her in my wings and nuzzling into the cloud of hair that is especially unruly in the mornings. She smells faintly of flowers and resin from her most recent project.

"We'll go to the Meadows today," I murmur into her curls, "but first, we should go back to the bedroom."

Sometimes we go to the Caverns, but we've learned each other's bodies well enough that it's not necessary anymore. Honestly, with the way we cannot get enough of each other, we'd have had to move to the Caverns if it was. Now we just go to play with the ropes every once in a while.

"I thought you'd never ask," she purrs, abandoning the rest of her *subus* with her camera to grab the collar of my shirt and pull me down for a kiss.

I lick her lips eagerly, and she parts them to give me access. The kiss deepens as she reaches up to caress my ear. When I groan into her mouth, she pulls back with a devious smile.

"Race you to the bedroom," she cackles, giving my chest a little shove that barely moves me before turning and running out of the kitchen.

Laughter pours out of me as I chase her, catching up to her as she passes through the bedroom door and scooping her up in my wings.

When I toss her onto the bed, she giggles, staring up at me with such trust and love it stops me in my tracks.

Only for a moment, though.

It's a beautiful day in the Meadows. It may be manufactured, but there's still weather in most of the biomes. This afternoon, though, it's bright, with a slight breeze, perfect for a flight or a picnic. Several other citizens must have had similar thoughts because the Meadows are buzzing with people.

When we pop in the barn for Hope to pick out a wind rider, there are already several familiar faces prepping the tall, colorful vehicles. Hope waves to Bazzel and her father, Jerrol, finally fully healed, as they push out their own wind riders. Behind them, Harrow walks with her arms folded across her chest. When she spots us, she pivots on her feet.

"Hope, I know you see me. Don't you try to run!"

Much to my amusement, Hope *was* trying to slip into the barn and avoid one of Harrow's intimidating lectures. She turns back bashfully when she realizes she's caught.

"Harrow, I would never run from you," she swears, "ma'am."

Just like I'd suspected, Harrow took Hope under her wing like her own kit. Unfortunately for Hope, that mostly means getting lectured, chastised and lightly insulted by the toughest Silfan on this space ship. It also means having the nosiest community watch member on our Division keeping an eye on you, getting "volun-told" into a lot of station activities, and being forced to go to their place for dinner every seven days.

Hope adores it. I can tell by the way her lips get this mischievous tilt to them whenever Harrow starts lecturing her, like she's contemplating how best to rebel against Harrow without pissing her off too much. Bazzel is thrilled to have her mom's attention elsewhere, and Harrow just loves to lord over everyone. I'm pretty sure Harrow is the only person Hope has ever been intimidated by. Frankly, it's been a beautiful thing to watch evolve.

"I thought I told you to stop by the house this week and help me with my poster for the conference," she berates my mate.

I can't help but snicker a little.

"You asked me that yesterday, Harrow. I'm going to come see you, I promise."

"What is the point of having an artist in the family if I can't have the best looking presentation on station security there is. Did you know that the Originem don't even have a forensics team on board here?" She informs us sternly.

"Have there ever been any instances where we've needed one?" Hope asks, sounding genuinely confused.

"No," I cut in. "The crime rate is virtually nonexistent, which is why the Originem don't waste resources on things like this."

"Better to have it and not need it..." Harrow grumbles, pointing a pink finger at me.

She may be half my size, but I'd be lying if I said she didn't intimidate me a bit, too. And it has nothing to do with the rumored defense mechanisms Silfans have.

"I'll come by after our flight today," Hope claims, drawing the tiny woman's attention back to her.

"Alright, well, you better. I'm making *dersial* stew." Satisfied by Hope's promises, Harrow stomps away.

"Alright, babe, we better make this fast. She doesn't like to fly, but I have no doubt Harrow will make an exception just to come fetch me," Hope says, already walking over to her favorite wind rider.

Between the two of us, we have it pulled out of the barn in no time. Hope insists on rolling it to the long, flat field they use as a runway, but most days she'll at least let me help her push. Taking off though? I'd be a fool to even offer my assistance. Instead, I lean down and kiss her softly.

"See you up there," I whisper before jumping and thrusting my wings down, shooting straight up into the air.

This isn't the first time we've been flying together, or even the second, but every time I still get a rush watching her pilot the wind rider with natural skill. The moment she leaves the ground, she always hollers with joy and I feel the swoop of my belly just like it were *me* defying gravity without wings.

Normally, Hope ascends quickly to meet me, but this time I can tell immediately something is wrong. She's only a few yards in the air when the wind rider dips dangerously. I immediately tuck into a dive, my heart pounding so fast I'm vibrating. She's already landed, albeit clumsily, far less gracefully than she usually does. My feet windmill before I hit the ground, desperate to run to my mate.

When I see her, red-faced and panting, my heart immediately eases. Only to speed right back up as I watch her vomit over the side of her rider. She's safe, she's whole, and there's only one reason I can think of why she would suddenly be puking.

"My Hope, my love, are you okay?" I implore as soon as I reach her, rubbing a claw gently across her back.

"Ugh, I don't know what came over me. I was fine all morning, but as soon as I left the ground it was like the worst case of carsick I've ever had," she tells me, wiping her mouth with the back of her sleeve.

"I think fate has finally decided," I murmur, emotions already threatening to clog my throat.

"What? What are you saying, Meshi?" Hope asks. To anyone else she would sound accusatory, but I know that she's just worried. Not that she'd ever admit it.

"Winged-One mothers get flight-sick when they are carrying a child. Something about their equilibrium being off, I'm not sure of the intricacies. We'll have to ask my mom," I explain as I keep gently stroking her back. Hope likes to have all the information. It helps her feel in control.

"Hoooly shit," she replies, looking up at me with wide eyes.

"Is that okay?" I ask tentatively. I know she said we could let fate decide, but we haven't discussed it much since then. I knew it was an inevitability, though, especially with all the rumors of several other human women being pregnant. Something about human females and males of other species just worked well together, it seemed.

"Yes it's okay, you goofball! It's crazy, but it's amazing, too." She curves an arm around her belly, looking down at it thoughtfully. "They're in there right now. Our baby."

Her face when she looks back up at me is full of such peace and contentment, such hope and joy, it almost brings me to my knees.

"I told you, Dad!" A voice carries from the far side of the field. Hope and I both look over to see Bazzel and Jerrol running towards us. "Why are you clutching your stomach, Hope?"

"Oh my gosh, seriously? Can no one have a moment of privacy on this space station?" Hope teases her friend, but there's no real heat in her voice.

"Absolutely not. Are you sick?" Bazzel asks, her voice laced with concern.

"Not sick," Hope replies. When she raises her eyebrows at me I nod my head encouragingly. "It's possible that Meshi and I are pregnant."

She says it's possible, but I know for sure. I can feel the rightness of it.

Bazzel wraps Hope in a hug as soon as she's close enough. Jerrol, right on his daughter's heels, pulls me in for one, as well.

"Congratulations, my friend. I am so happy for you," he mutters, then raises his voice to address Hope. "You two better go tell Harrow. If she finds out from anyone else, you will never hear the end of it, and I'm pretty sure every Winged-One in the sky saw you dive-bomb for your mate a moment ago, Meshi."

Hope snickers, but she nods along in agreement.

"You're right. She's already threatened me once this morning. We'll head there now."

Bazzel and Jerrol agree to take the wind rider back to the barn and Hope wastes no time grabbing my hand and pulling me towards the exit. The instant camera knocks against my sternum, forgotten until just now.

"What about your last picture?" I inquire, gesturing towards the clunky thing hanging around my neck.

"Let's save it. We'll take it when we're all together. Our family."

Epilogue: Josep

A few months later

"So the human women have started a support group," Lokas murmurs, lifting his mug to sip at his steaming *subus.*

"Yes, I heard. That's good," I reply, sipping my own warm drink.

The humans have changed things on this station so much already. Lokas and I both have been stationed here for over two decades, but we only recently discovered the warm drink. Its popularity among humans is spreading throughout the rest of the station like wildfire. Now they're starting support groups and mentor programs, all things we should have been doing for them, but we had different orders.

"Is it not...counterintuitive to our orders, sir?" he asks, hesitatingly. "I thought we wanted them to be isolated and lonely, so they have to reach out to the other citizens?"

I narrow my eyes at him across the table.

"I know you're the one who put the idea in her head. Don't try to play me for the fool," I inform him, but in truth I'm not upset at all by his antics. "In fact, I was perhaps trying to help in my own way, as well. I do have a little insider knowledge on earthlings. After all, I was stationed there many, many years ago."

"Oh, I always forget about that! So you gave your maintenance men dating advice? Is that it?" Lokas chuckles, shaking his head. "We're terrible at following orders, aren't we?"

"I think we've done nothing but advance the Originem's overall goal. There are no less than five citizens pregnant with hybrid children at this point and the entire station has accepted this almost seamlessly. It's better than they could have even hoped," I assure Lokas.

"Do you think they'll hate us when they find out?" His voice wavers, and I put a comforting hand on his arm—another human gesture I've picked up. Originem are not very "touchy-feely" as a species.

"I ask myself this often, my friend," I confess. "I can only hope they will see all the good that has come from this, that we only ever wanted what was best for everyone."

He still looks pained, staring across the small cafe where a group of human women are seated in a circle of cushions on the ground. They all have mugs clutched in their hands and smiles on their faces. From this distance, it's impossible to see, but a few have also been observed to have the beginnings of baby bumps. Joy and envy fill my lungs in equal measure. I'm elated for Meshi, Khur and my other friends who are starting their families, but I have to wonder, when will it be my turn?

"I made sure they only sent women who wanted to have children, women who were open to the idea of starting a family, who had flexible, broadminded perceptions on love and life. We did extensive testing, and the few bad seeds we had to let through, like that awful father on division five, are weeding themselves out. Everything is working out perfectly, for everyone," I reassure him, as well as myself. "I think they'll understand, in the end."

Acknowledgements

This book is first and foremost for my sister. Thank you for supporting me in everything I do and laughing at all my terrible jokes. Thank you for challenging me and always keeping me humble. Tell the kids that if Yaya can write books, they can do anything!

To my husband, during the many long nights this book kept me out of bed, thank you for pulling me in.

To Lorna Grimm, our completely unhinged conversations molded this book into the beauty that it is. I'm so glad we get to be authors together.

Mom and Dad. I still hope you don't ever read this, but if you do, I want to say you did a really good job. You encouraged me to follow my dreams my entire life, and even though it took about 34 years, you celebrated it all the same. Even when I wouldn't let you read it. Thank you.

Finally, my readers. Thank you for sticking with me on this journey. I will strive to keep writing stories that are worthy of you.

Happy reading, darlings.

About the Author

Rhea Ridge writes love stories that cross galaxies and realms. When she's not imagining scenarios where humans get to kiss aliens, she's drinking lavender lattes and reading any book she can get her hands on. She lives in Kentucky with her husband and their spoiled, senior cats.

www.ingramcontent.com/pod-product-compliance
Lightning Source LLC
LaVergne TN
LVHW020716110826
845149LV00012B/2290

* 9 7 9 8 9 9 9 7 2 2 7 2 0 *